Freedom Run

Freedom Run

Paul McCusker

PUBLISHING
Colorado Springs, Colorado

FREEDOM RUN

Library of Congress Cataloging-in-Publication Data
McCusker, Paul, 1958-
    Freedom Run / Paul McCusker.
        p.   cm.—(Adventures in Odyssey; 10)
    Summary: Jack and Matt use The Imagination Station to travel back in
time again to the pre-Civil War South, where they plan to carry out their
promise to help two slaves escape through the Underground Railroad.
    ISBN 1-56179-475-9
    [1. Underground railroad—Fiction. 2. Fugitive slaves—Fiction.
3. Slavery—Fiction. 4. Time travel—Fiction. 5. Afro-Americans—Fiction.]
I. Title. II. Series: McCusker, Paul 1958-   Adventures in Odyssey; 10.
PZ7.M47841635Fr 1996
[Fic]—dc20   96-25908
                                                      CIP
                                                      AC
Published by Focus on the Family Publishing, Colorado Springs, CO 80995.

Distributed in the U.S.A. and Canada by Word Books, Dallas, Texas.

The author is represented by the literary agency of Alive Communications,
1465 Kelly Johnson Blvd., Suite 320, Colorado Springs, CO 80920.

This is a work of fiction, and any resemblance between the characters in this
book and real persons is coincidental.

Editor: Larry K. Weeden
Front cover illustration: JoAnn Weistling
Printed in the United States of America

97 98 99/10 9 8 7 6 5 4 3 2

Adventures in Odyssey Novel 10: Freedom Run

With special acknowledgment to
Marshal Younger and his Underground Railroad
episodes for the "Adventures in Odyssey"
radio series.

INTRODUCTION

My name's John Avery Whittaker, though a lot of folks around Odyssey call me Whit. I own a soda shop and "discovery emporium" called Whit's End. I guess you could say it's like a cross between an ice cream parlor and an interactive museum. Whit's End has room after room of displays, games, books, and activities so the kids who come to visit will have fun while learning important lessons at the same time.

One room the kids aren't generally allowed to visit is my workshop down in the basement. That's where I design and experiment with the inventions that eventually wind up in one of the rooms upstairs. The place is packed with half-finished ideas and machines that could be dangerous if they weren't handled correctly. That's why I ask the kids to keep out.

One crisp fall day, Jack Davis and Matthew Booker—two boys who come to Whit's End a lot—were playing in the woods behind my shop. They stumbled on a door in the ground. Even though a sign said to "Keep Out," Jack and Matt went through the door and wound up in a tunnel that leads to my workshop.

You might think it's a little strange having a tunnel like that, but I learned it was once part of the Underground Railroad. In case you don't know, the Underground Railroad was a secret network of people who helped slaves to escape from the South to Canada in the years before the Civil War. Like a real railroad, it had "stops" along the way.

It turns out that part of the building that's now Whit's End was once a church run by a pastor named the Reverend Andrew. He helped the Underground Railroad by being one of those "stops." The tunnel was a secret passageway to get slaves in and out of the basement of the church, where the pastor took care of them. He gave them a place to sleep, new clothes, and food.

Jack and Matt found the tunnel and followed it to my workshop, where they came upon one of my inventions—a machine called The Imagination Station. I created it to help make the Bible and all of history come to life for whoever gets in. (I'd explain how it works, but it's too technical and boring.) I wasn't there at the time, but I had left The Imagination Station's computers on to input information for one of the adventures I'd created. That particular day, I had been working on a program about the Underground Railroad and some of the people who came through it.

You can probably guess what happened. Jack and Matt got into The Imagination Station. I believe Matt said later that he thought it was some kind of "ride." It sure was! No sooner had the boys pushed the red button to start the machine than they found themselves stuck in the Odyssey *of 1858*.

Part of what happened to them there can be found in a book called *Dark Passage*. In short, the two boys were caught in a chase after a runaway slave named Clarence and his daughter, Eveline. Because Matt is black, he was captured by some slave hunters, who took him south to Alabama with Clarence and Eveline. Jack and the Reverend Andrew followed with a scheme to help them escape to the North again.

You can imagine how scared Matt and Jack were, since they had been trapped in a frightening Imagination Station adventure and didn't know how to get out.

In a strange twist to the story, Matt and Eveline were sold at a slave auction to one slave owner, while Clarence was sold to another. Eveline was terribly upset to be separated from her father like that. Matt bravely promised that he'd help her get back to him somehow.

I returned to my workshop and was surprised to find the two boys in The Imagination Station. I immediately turned off the machine. Jack was relieved to get out, but, to my surprise, Matt was in tears. I had stopped the adventure right after he had promised to help Eveline find her father.

To make matters worse, we realized Clarence and Eveline were never *supposed* to be separated. In their original story, they had both been sold together, then later escaped north again. But their story had changed because Jack and Matt got into The Imagination Station right in the middle of the computer's programming. I figured the computer was confused by the interference and, as a result, changed the story completely. This made Matt and Jack feel even worse, since they thought they were responsible for messing up Clarence and Eveline's lives. It was all so real to them.

They asked me to let them finish the adventure so Matt could keep his promise to Eveline and Jack could help the Reverend Andrew as he had said he would. How could I say no?

As part of the boys' "punishment" for getting into my workroom (and The Imagination Station) without permission, I made them write down the rest of their adventure. I polished it up a little, fixed the spelling, and edited it so readers can follow who is telling what part of the story where and . . . well, you'll see.

They wanted to call it *Jack's and Matt's Big Adventure*, but they got in a loud argument over whose name should go first. So I suggested we call it *Freedom Run* as a follow-up to *Dark Passage*.

I'll stop taking up your time now and let the boys tell their own stories.

—John Avery Whittaker

CHAPTER ONE

Matt tells about the plantation.

I scooted over in the seat as Jack squeezed next to me in The Imagination Station. He didn't say anything. I was glad. Nothing a guy hates worse than to have his best friend make a fuss about the fact that he was crying. I turned away and rubbed my eyes. I hoped my nose wouldn't run. It always runs when I cry, and I didn't have a tissue.

It was kind of dumb to get so upset, I know. But I felt bad about promising to help Eveline find her father and then—*zing*—all of a sudden I was yanked out of the slave wagon and brought back to my time. Don't get me wrong, I was happy to be home. I didn't think we'd *ever* get back. I hated being a black kid in a world where everyone thought blacks were good only for being slaves. I hated being treated worse than an animal. I wanted to get back to *my* Odyssey, where people treated me like . . . well, *me*.

But poor Eveline was stuck back there on that wagon without her father, and it was *my* fault in a way. If Jack and I hadn't gotten into The Imagination Station in the first place, things would've turned out the way they were supposed to. I mean, what could I do except go back and try to fix everything? What would *you* do?

"Just push the red button when you're ready," Mr. Whittaker said as the door to The Imagination Station *whooshed* shut. The lights on the panel blinked at us like a Christmas tree.

"We have to be out of our minds to go back," Jack said.

"Yeah, we probably are," I answered.

Jack reached over and pushed down on the flashing red button.

The machine hummed louder and louder until it felt as if it had suddenly jumped forward. I had the same feeling in the pit of my stomach that I get on a roller-coaster ride, or in the car when my dad hits a dip in the road too fast. It turned my stomach upside down and sucked the breath out of me. Everything went dark. For a minute, I wasn't sure where I was. Then I smelled old straw and heard the clip-clop of horses' hooves and the slow creaking of a wooden wagon. I guessed that somehow The Imagination Station had put me right back where I was before. Only now I was half-buried in a pile of straw. I sat up, and my body ached all over. I had forgotten about being knocked around by Mr. Ramsay's overseer and kicked by the man at the slave auction.

"Are you all right?" Eveline asked. The tears were still in

her eyes, but now they were wide like she'd just seen a ghost.

"I'm all right," I said. I had no idea what had happened—if I had suddenly disappeared right in front of her when The Imagination Station took me back to my time, if I had just reappeared, or what. "Why?"

She watched me carefully. "You rolled under the hay all of a sudden. Were you afraid of something?"

"I . . . I . . ." I couldn't think of an answer that would make sense. "Never mind."

"You were crying, weren't you?" Eveline said softly.

Oh, brother, I thought.

"You two better shut your traps!" the wagon driver growled. He was a heavyset man named Master Kinsey. He was the overseer, the man in charge of the slaves, at Colonel Ross's plantation. "A few days in the field will take the spunk out of you," he threatened.

I believed him. But Colonel Ross was the owner of the plantation, and he had other ideas.

My mother once made me watch a movie called *Gone with the Wind.* I didn't like it much, because it was long and boring and all about a woman who didn't care who she hurt as long as she got what she wanted. There was a big fire in it, which was okay, but other than that, the adults can have it. Anyway, Colonel Ross lived in a house like the one in the movie. It was real big, with large windows and giant pillars along the front. Master Kinsey pulled the wagon around the back, where the sheds and barns were. Beyond them was a "compound" of shacks where the slaves lived. And beyond that was a field that went way out to the horizon.

The place was so pretty that I was beginning to think it might not be so bad there after all. Then I remembered that I wasn't there as a visitor, I was a *slave*. How could I ever forget it?

A wiry black man in a dark butler-type suit hustled down the stairs from the back door and raced to the wagon. He was out of breath with excitement. "Saints be blessed, they're here," he said.

I looked around to see who he was talking about and was surprised to realize that it was me and Eveline.

"You can just forget about it, Jonah," Master Kinsey said. "I'm putting them in the fields."

Jonah waved his arms around nervously. "No, sir, Master Kinsey," he said. "Colonel Ross said they're for the house. You can ask him yourself, they're for the house."

Master Kinsey punched the seat of the wagon. "You can be sure I will, you old liar," he declared. He leapt down from the wagon with a loud grunt and marched into the house.

"I'm Jonah," he said to me and Eveline. "Now come down from the wagon, young'uns. Let me have a look at you." We jumped down, and the jolt made my ribs hurt all over again. He circled us to get a good look. "I think little Nell's old clothes'll fit you," he said to Eveline. Then he eyed me up and down. "Nate's will do for you."

"Won't Nate mind me taking his clothes?" I asked.

"He might mind if he were here and still wanting to wear them," Jonah said.

"Where is he?" I asked.

"Got shot trying to run away."

The back door slammed. Master Kinsey stomped down the stairs, muttering, "He spoils these slaves, I tell you! You don't break them in and you have nothing but trouble from them." He climbed back onto the wagon, swearing and fuming, and slapped the reins for the horse to get moving.

Jonah smiled. "I reckon the Colonel told him. You're to work in the house with me."

Jonah led us into the back of the house to the kitchen. It was a massive room, with a big, wooden table in the middle and a gigantic fireplace off to the side that someone had bricked up. Nearby sat an enormous cast-iron stove. A woman was fussing over the stove, trying to get a fire started in it. The walls were lined with shelves covered with plates and bowls. Pots and pans hung from the ceiling.

Jonah called out to the woman to say that the new house servants were here. "Looky here, Lizzie!"

She waved at us without a lot of interest and returned to the stove.

A sturdy-looking beagle strolled into the kitchen to see what was going on. Jonah and Lizzie watched it nervously. "That's Scout," Jonah said. "Don't try to pet him, he'll take your hand off. He don't like slaves much."

"He doesn't? Why not?" I asked as I tucked my hands under my arms and froze where I was. Scout sniffed at me.

"He's trained to catch runaways," Jonah replied.

Scout turned to Eveline.

"You're a pretty dog," she said and reached down to scratch him behind his ears. I braced myself for an attack. But to everyone's surprise, Scout closed his eyes and panted happily.

"Well, look at that," Jonah said.

I breathed a sigh of relief.

Jonah waved at us to follow him up a narrow flight of stairs. At the top were a couple of rooms. He gestured to the one on the right and said, "That's my room. You're in this one." He pushed open a dried up, scarred, wooden door.

"We have our own room?" Eveline asked.

"You want us to *share* a room?" I asked. I couldn't believe it.

Jonah went on as if he didn't hear me. "It's got its own window and two beds . . ."

Two *cots,* he meant.

Eveline raced over to one and dropped onto it. Dust flew everywhere. She bounced around as if she'd just been given a bed at the White House or something. I didn't get it. They were two cots with ratty blankets on top. I kind of snorted to show I wasn't impressed.

"I'm not gonna sleep on *that,*" I said.

Jonah suddenly grabbed my arm and leaned into my face. His eyes had a yellow color, and his breath smelled of old cabbage. "Look, *boy,*" he said, "you could be sleeping out in the compound with no bed and no blanket and working in the fields until you want to drop. You better thank the Lord you're in here. Got it?"

I nodded my head up and down real fast.

He let go, but he kept a stern tone in his voice. "Let me tell you how things are around here. You're house servants, and that means you have to behave. You do what I say, stay out of the master's way, and everything'll be good. Step the wrong way and you'll be licking Master Kinsey's boots."

"But we never liked the house slaves," Eveline said. She didn't mean anything by it but said it as a matter of fact.

"You've been a field slave, haven't you?" Jonah asked.

Eveline nodded.

Jonah hitched his thumbs in his pockets. "Well, I know field slaves don't trust us house slaves. That's how it is in some places. And I know some house slaves I wouldn't trust neither. But let me tell you that around here, we house slaves watch out for the ones working in the fields. So don't give me an attitude."

Eveline nodded again. For her, the case was closed.

It wasn't for Jonah. He continued, "I know the field slaves think we house slaves have it easy as pie. But we don't. You'll see that soon enough. You'll run errands, go to the market, work in the garden, milk the cows, serve meals, help take care of the horses, dust the house, sweep up, polish the silver, and set the table in the dining room. As a house slave, you're always on duty—the master may call anytime, day or night. You're the last one to bed and the first one to rise."

I got tired just listening to him talk about all the work I'd do. The only thing that kept me hopeful was that I had come back to help Eveline find her father—and then we'd all escape. The only problem was that I didn't know *how* we'd do it.

I wondered where Jack was—and if he and Reverend Andrew had come up with a plan.

CHAPTER TWO

Jack tells about the bird-watcher.

Reverend Andrew wasn't Reverend Andrew anymore. He got rid of his clerical collar and all his antislavery stuff and became Andrew Ferguson, a bird-watcher who was touring through the South to draw and collect all kinds of birds. I was his assistant. I called him "Uncle Andrew."

I guess I should explain that when Mr. Whittaker turned off The Imagination Station, I had been sitting in a chair in our hotel room in Huntsville, Alabama. Uncle Andrew was washing his face. He had just scolded me for not keeping my mouth shut when he was talking to the slave trader at the auction about where Eveline and Matt had been taken. I was moping and complaining when the butterflies suddenly went crazy in my stomach—and the next thing I knew, I was with Mr. Whittaker again. It was so weird because when I pushed the red button to go back to the adventure, The Imagination Station put me right where I left off in that hotel room. It was like hitting the pause button on a video player, then starting it again.

Uncle Andrew turned around to me from the washstand and asked, "What did you say?"

I felt embarrassed because I couldn't remember what I had said. I just shrugged.

"This evening we're going to the Mason plantation for dinner," Uncle Andrew explained.

I sat up in my chair. "The Mason plantation? But Matt and Eveline are at Colonel Ross's plantation!"

Uncle Andrew turned to face me. "How did you know that?" he asked.

His question made my brain seize up. *How did I know?* "You told me, didn't you?" I finally managed.

"The slave auctioneer told *me,* but I don't remember telling *you.*"

"You must have told me," I gulped. "How else could I know?"

The question must've stumped him, because he didn't answer or ask me again.

"Anyway," Uncle Andrew went on, "we're going to the Masons'. I had already arranged it through my friend before we arrived. Mr. Mason is interested in ornithology."

"What's that mean again?" I asked.

"It's the study of birds."

"That's right," I said. "I keep thinking it's those dentists who put braces on teeth."

Uncle Andrew shot me a strange look but didn't say anything.

"So when are we going over to Colonel Ross's to rescue Matt and Eveline?" I asked.

"In due time," Uncle Andrew said firmly. "Our purpose here isn't just to rescue them. We have to help spread the word among the slaves about the Underground Railroad."

"Spread the word about it? Don't they know already?"

"No, many of them don't. Many of them are so isolated on the plantations that they have no way of knowing." Uncle Andrew dabbed a towel at his face. "And it'll be a lot easier to get to the slaves if I can build up a friendship with some of the plantation owners."

I knew that being impatient wouldn't help anything, so I agreed to do whatever Uncle Andrew wanted. I regretted it right away when he handed me a stiff suit with a collar like cardboard that cut into my neck.

"If we're going to a dinner party, you have to *dress* for a dinner party," he said with a smile.

We hired a carriage to take us out to the Mason plantation just as the sun was going down. It must've taken us a half hour to get there, and I was completely lost. I wondered out loud how the slaves ever knew which way to escape.

Uncle Andrew checked to make sure the driver couldn't hear us, then pointed out the carriage window to the sky. "The north star," he said. "We tell them to follow the north star."

We turned onto a dirt driveway, where flickering lamps showed us the way to the Mason house. It was a mansion built in what Uncle Andrew said was the Greek Revival style of architecture, which was real popular then. I assumed he was talking about the large, white pillars along the front porch.

A servant ran down to meet our carriage and helped us out. I said, "Thanks," but he didn't look at me or say anything. We strolled up to the front door, which was actually two *massive* doors, and another servant let us in. (Maybe I should mention that all the servants were black.)

We stepped through the front door, and I have to tell you: This place was *huge*. It had a front hall you could've played basketball in. Off of that, the widest staircase I'd ever seen curved around up to the second floor. There were paintings of people all over the walls. The furniture was that rich, curlicue kind, with round backs on the chairs and legs that curve in and out. The house was full of fancy tables, gigantic mirrors, and sparkling chandeliers. Uncle Andrew pointed out that the chandeliers were "Waterford" and the furniture represented the Empire, Victorian, and Early American periods. All I know is I never saw anything like it at Sears.

I tugged at my collar and felt out of place. *It's going to be a long night,* I thought.

A tall man with a white beard and a woman with big curls in her hair came out to meet us. "Welcome to our home!" the man said as if he meant it. His hand was stuck out for Uncle Andrew to shake. He did. "I'm Richard Mason. This is my wife, Annabelle."

Annabelle curtsied.

"A pleasure to meet you," Uncle Andrew said, then

bowed like a gentleman to Mrs. Mason. "I'd like you to meet my assistant, Jack."

Remembering Uncle Andrew's warning, I made sure to keep my mouth shut except to say, "It's very nice to meet you."

Uncle Andrew said, "Thank you for opening your home to us so graciously."

Mr. Mason clapped Uncle Andrew on the back. "When John said you were coming to our fair town, I insisted you join us for a meal. Didn't I, Annabelle?"

"You certainly did," Annabelle said softly.

"Come into the living room," Mr. Mason said and led the way.

It was another gigantic room with a lot of fancy furniture and a huge, carved-wood fireplace. Uncle Andrew made a fuss over the "Chippendale mirror" above the "rosewood piano" and the authentic "French porcelain mantel clock." His compliments charmed the socks off both Mr. and Mrs. Mason.

"I take it from your accent that you're from Britain," Mr. Mason said after we were all sitting down.

"England," Uncle Andrew clarified.

"A Johnny Bull! I have family in Runnymede," Mr. Mason exclaimed.

"Oh, please, Richard, they're hardly family," Mrs. Mason said. "Distant cousins at best. Please, Mr. Ferguson—"

"Andrew," he corrected her.

It looked to me as if she blushed. "*Andrew.* Tell us about your purpose here."

Uncle Andrew sat up proudly and told them all about the studies he wanted to do of the birds in the area and how he hoped to catch a few to take back north. I noticed that just saying the word *north* made Mr. and Mrs. Mason stiffen.

Mr. Mason said, "Tell me, sir, if all northerners are opposed to slavery."

"Not all," Uncle Andrew replied honestly.

Mrs. Mason fanned herself as if she were too hot. "I shudder to think of the abolitionists who would wreak violence on us all."

"I take it, sir, that you are not of that mind," Mr. Mason said.

It felt as though my collar shrunk around my neck while I waited for Uncle Andrew to answer.

He smiled politely and said, "Would I be here now if I were?"

The servant who had let us in the front door suddenly appeared to say that dinner was served in the dining room. I was so relieved by the interruption that I nearly leapt to my feet.

Uncle Andrew frowned at me.

"Hungry, boy?" Mr. Mason said with a chuckle.

"Yes, sir." I smiled in my most angelic way.

"Then let's not dillydally!" Mr. Mason said.

During dinner—which was chicken, potatoes, and a green kind of vegetable I didn't recognize—Mr. Mason told us all about his grown-up sons who'd become successful lawyers and merchants in other parts of the South. Mrs.

Mason beamed while he spoke. I watched them both while I ate and wondered how such nice people could *buy and sell* other human beings as slaves. It didn't make sense. Every time the servants came into the dining room to make sure we were okay, I had to remind myself they weren't just waiters in some restaurant—they were *owned* and didn't have a choice about whether they wanted to be there.

Eventually Uncle Andrew steered the conversation back to birds and talked about his desire to spend time in the surrounding countryside, drawing and cataloging the native species. Mr. Mason took the hint and told Uncle Andrew he was more than welcome to bird-watch *their* property.

"In fact, I'm an amateur bird-watcher myself," Mr. Mason said. "I'm familiar with the works of Wilson. Wilson was from your country, wasn't he?"

I had a feeling that Mr. Mason was testing Uncle Andrew.

"If you mean Alexander Wilson, he was from Scotland," Uncle Andrew replied easily. "His nine-volume work *American Ornithology* was unsurpassed. That is, until Audubon published *his* definitive *Birds of America.*"

Mr. Mason knew his bluff had been called. "Yes, an excellent work. In any event, if it won't be intrusive, I might come along with you tomorrow!" Mr. Mason exclaimed.

I dropped my fork, and it hit the plate with a deafening clang.

Uncle Andrew smiled and said, "That would be delightful!"

Mrs. Mason cleared her throat. "Richard," she said,

"you're supposed to go into town tomorrow, remember?"

"Oh, blast it all!" Mr. Mason shouted. "That confounded meeting with the bankers. You're right, of course."

"Oh, too bad. Some other time perhaps," Uncle Andrew said.

A droplet of sweat tickled at the back of my neck.

"If you need anyone else to assist you, besides your young companion here, I'll be happy for one of my servants to accompany you," Mr. Mason offered.

Uncle Andrew said he was most kind. And as everyone was distracted by their plates of food again, he winked at me.

CHAPTER THREE

Jack tells about bird-watching.

N ow, tell me how one identifies birds," Uncle Andrew asked the next day as we tramped across a field not far from Mason's house.

It was a pop quiz. Just that morning, he had lectured me about how to be a bird-watcher. He said that if I was going to be his assistant, I had to at least sound as if I knew what I was talking about.

I tried to think as I adjusted the sack hanging from my shoulder. In it were Uncle Andrew's pads of paper, pens, and watercolors so he could sketch some of the birds we hoped to find. "The marks around the eyes . . ." I said.

"And?"

I thought again. "The marks on their wings . . ."

"Very good. And what else?"

My mind was blank, so I guessed. "The color of their beaks?"

Uncle Andrew shook his head. "I suppose the *shape* of their beaks might be helpful, even the color. But you guessed the wrong end. The correct answer is the marks on their outer tail feathers."

I frowned. "Oh, yeah."

We reached the edge of some woods, and Uncle Andrew stopped. He pointed to a cavity in a nearby tree. "There."

I looked up but didn't see what he was pointing at.

"See? The Eastern bluebird."

My eyes finally fixed on a bright-blue bird with an orangey chest sitting on a branch. Another bird just like it flew in from the field and landed on the branch. The high-pitched chirps from the tree said it was a mom and dad watching over a nest.

"Do you want to draw them?" I asked.

"No, I've sketched some of them from a previous trip. But I wanted you to see them for yourself. That way, if anyone asks, you can say what kind of bird you saw and give a reasonable description."

"Eastern bluebird," I repeated.

"Come along," he said and continued into the woods.

"Where are we going?"

Uncle Andrew said softly, "These woods circle Mason's plantation. I want to stroll around the perimeter, then 'accidentally' come upon the fields where the slaves will be working. Lord willing, I'll have a chance to talk to them."

We walked through the woods, and every once in a while, Uncle Andrew would stop to sketch on his pad, or he'd point out different birds to me. Eventually we got to the edge of a field. In the distance, we could see a group of slaves clearing the field. An overseer sat nearby and barked orders at them.

"Set up my easel here," Uncle Andrew said. "I'll go have a word with the overseer so he won't chase us off."

I nodded and started to unpack the bag while he strode across the field in large steps. I had just set up the wooden legs of the easel when I heard the clanging of several bells. At first, I thought it might be the cook signaling everyone that it was time for lunch, so I didn't pay attention. But the clanging came closer and closer, so I looked up. Three slaves were carrying a huge log away from the field and toward the woods. Two of the slaves looked the way the slaves normally looked, but the third had something on his head that looked like a large helmet. As they walked past with the log, I saw it better and noticed that the thing wasn't a helmet as much as a kind of cage. It had a circle of iron around the top of the slave's head, with several rods fixed to it that stretched down to another circle of iron that fit around the slave's neck. It was fastened shut by a large padlock at the throat. There were big bells hanging from the rods that knocked around to make the clanging I heard.

I know my mouth fell open. The cage-helmet looked incredibly heavy, and I couldn't imagine how the slave was able to walk at all, let alone carry a log. The slave turned to me as they walked by, and I recognized him right away. It was Clarence, Eveline's father!

I wanted to shout, but Uncle Andrew's hand was on my shoulder. "I know," he said quietly. "Don't do anything that will draw attention to our knowledge."

I got busy with the easel again. "What was that thing on his head?" I asked.

"It's a way to punish slaves who've run away. They have to wear them day and night."

"It looks awful."

Uncle Andrew nodded. "It's worse than awful. With one of those contraptions on your head, you can barely stoop to work without straining all the muscles in your neck and shoulders. You can't put your head down to sleep—you have to crouch all night. But it serves its purpose. You can't run away without everyone hearing you." Uncle Andrew rubbed at his face, and I realized he was trying to get rid of the tears in his eyes.

"What are we going to do?"

"It's imperative we don't let on that we know Clarence."

"Okay."

Uncle Andrew rubbed his chin. "I think I have an idea."

Clarence and the two slaves threw the log into the woods, then came past us again. Uncle Andrew called out as he ran to them. The slaves looked stricken that this strange white man would approach like that. If Clarence recognized Uncle Andrew, he didn't let on.

"Pardon me," Uncle Andrew said, "but I'm doing some research on birds in this area."

The slaves shuffled their feet and looked anxiously

toward the overseer, who now stood up and watched the scene from across the field.

"I believe one of you is named Clarence."

Clarence said reluctantly, "That's me, sir."

"I've been told that you know a thing or two about birds. Is that true?"

"Well, sir . . ." Clarence spoke slowly, as if he weren't sure what the right answer was. "I know a thing or two about birds. Yes, sir."

"Hey!" the overseer shouted as he came closer.

"I may need some help with my research," Uncle Andrew said to Clarence.

The overseer was only a few yards away. "What's going on here?" he demanded. "You three—get back to work!"

"Yes, sir," the slaves said and rushed away. Clarence staggered behind, with the bells on his helmet ringing and clanging.

"You can look at birds all you want, but stay away from the slaves," the overseer said. "Distracts them from their work."

"I'm terribly sorry. It wasn't my intention to stir up trouble. But I'd like to talk to Mr. Mason about the one in the helmet."

"Why? What'd he do wrong?"

"Not a thing. I believe he may be of some assistance to us."

"Not that one. You can believe me."

"Jack, pack up our things," Uncle Andrew instructed. "Let's go to the mansion and have a word with Mr. Mason."

****

The servant showed us in to the study, where Mr. Mason was seated at the desk. He rose to greet us. "How was the bird-watching today?" he asked.

"Slightly disappointing," Uncle Andrew answered. "We're having trouble tracking the little devils."

"I was certain that a man of your expertise would have no trouble finding the birds he wanted."

Uncle Andrew bowed modestly. "You esteem me too highly. I'm a rank amateur. However, there is someone in your service who may be of great help to me."

"Is there? Who?"

"One of your slaves."

"I'm astounded," Mr. Mason said. "I'm not aware that any of my slaves would have a special knowledge of birds."

"It's obviously a knowledge from experience rather than books—of working the land and knowing the birds of the area as a result."

Mr. Mason shrugged. "Well, sir, if you want to borrow one of my slaves for a day's expedition, I don't mind. Which one is he?"

"The one with the unusual contraption on his head," Uncle Andrew said.

"Contraption?"

Uncle Andrew explained, "It looked like a cage with bells on it. Makes an infernal noise, I confess."

Mr. Mason thought for a moment, then realized whom

Uncle Andrew meant. "You're talking about one of my new slaves. I'm sorry, sir, but I'm not sure it would be prudent to let him wander the countryside with you."

"I agree, sir," Uncle Andrew said carefully. "Particularly with that commotion on his head. I don't think the birds would stay still with him banging and clamoring like he does."

Mr. Mason frowned. "Do you know why that boy is wearing that hat with the bells? It's because he runs away. I bought him from Ramsay because Ramsay was tired of dealing with him. I apologize, but if I take off the helmet, there'll be no stopping him from running away again."

"What if I were to promise that he wouldn't? What if I took full responsibility for him while he's with me?" Uncle Andrew locked his gaze on Mason and waited patiently for an answer.

Mr. Mason thought about it for a few moments, then shook his head. "I don't believe that would be a good idea. Not without the helmet."

"Perhaps we could take him with the helmet and the key to the padlock. If the bells scare off the birds, we can remove the helmet. If not, we'll leave it on."

It was a reasonable offer Mr. Mason couldn't refuse without looking as if he didn't trust us. "If you'll take responsibility for him and use discretion in your choice, then how can I protest? When would you like to take him?"

"Tomorrow, if you don't mind."

****

Later, as we walked to the carriage, I had to ask Uncle Andrew, "Does Clarence really know about birds, or did you make it up?"

Uncle Andrew didn't smile, but there was laughter in his voice. "I haven't the foggiest idea," he said. "I suspect he knows as much about birds as you do."

"Uh oh."

CHAPTER FOUR

Jack tells about a plan.

I don't like it. I don't like it one bit," the overseer—a man named Hickocks—complained as he gave us the key to Clarence's padlock.

"You worry too much," Mr. Mason said.

"You pay me to worry too much," Hickocks replied gruffly. "This buck'll run the first chance he gets."

"And I'll take responsibility for it if he does," Uncle Andrew said. "Unless you don't consider me a man of my word."

It was a challenge, and Hickocks seemed to know it. With muttered curses, he turned and walked off to a group of slaves who were waiting for him. "What are you standing around for, you good-for-nothings!" he shouted at them. Then he gestured for Clarence to join us.

"Hickocks is a little protective of our property," Mr.

Mason said apologetically.

At the word *property,* I looked hard at Mr. Mason. I wanted to say, "What do you mean by calling them property? They're *not* your property. They don't belong to *anybody.* And you have no right to think so." The words were right on the tip of my tongue, but I bit them back.

Clarence walked up to us with the bells on his hat banging away.

"Our guest seems to think you know a thing or two about birds," Mr. Mason told him.

Clarence wouldn't look Mr. Mason in the eye, but he gave him a slight nod and said, "Yes, sir."

Mr. Mason held up a finger. "I'm entrusting you to Mr. Ferguson. If you try to run away, not only will I be sorely put out, but so will Mr. Ferguson. Between the two of us, I reckon we'll catch you and hang you in a most painful way. Do you understand?"

"Yes, sir."

"Good bird-hunting, then," Mr. Mason said.

We thanked him for his kindness and strolled with Clarence across the field and into the nearest patch of woods. Clarence did his best to keep his head still so the bells wouldn't clang, but it was no use. It sounded as though a herd of cows with bells around their necks was on a stampede.

"We'll have to walk far enough away so they can't hear the bells," Uncle Andrew said.

Mr. Mason owned a lot of land, so we made it pretty far before Uncle Andrew stopped and faced Clarence directly.

"We'll never find any birds like this," he said.

"Are we really looking for birds, sir?" Clarence asked.

"Only the kind to set free," Uncle Andrew replied, then produced the key to the helmet. "Is it safe?"

"We should be clear of the farm," Clarence said.

"I've been watching behind us to make sure no one was following," I said, proud of myself for thinking to do it.

"Good lad," Uncle Andrew said, then grabbed the padlock at the base of the helmet. "Let's get that thing off your head."

"Are you sure, sir? I mean, this whole thing seems risky to me," Clarence said with a worried sound in his voice.

Uncle Andrew nodded. "I'm sure."

The lock was a little rusty, and it took a minute or two to get the key moving inside it. I was afraid Hickocks gave us the wrong key. (I wouldn't have put it past him to do something like that.) Finally, something clicked, and the lock came loose. We helped Clarence take the helmet off. Clarence immediately moved his head to the left, then to the right, then rolled it around and around on his shoulders. Each movement made him groan with pain.

With a victorious shout, Uncle Andrew and I threw the helmet into a pile of leaves.

"Cover it up, Jack," Uncle Andrew said.

I grabbed leaves and started to bury the ugly thing.

"What are you doing? I have to take it back!" Clarence said.

Uncle Andrew brushed his hands off. "I promised to bring *you* back, not that inhumane piece of iron."

Clarence reached out to Uncle Andrew. "Look, Reverend, forget about me. But I beg you to go to Colonel Ross's house and get my little girl. That's where she is. Your friend, too. It's only six miles away. Jake told me—he goes there on errands. He saw them with his own eyes."

"I won't forget about you, Clarence," Uncle Andrew said firmly. "If all goes according to plan, tomorrow night we'll *all* leave together."

"Tomorrow night? But how?"

"Yeah—goes according to *what* plan?" I asked.

Uncle Andrew smiled. "The plan I'm making up as we go along."

"Oh, Lord have mercy," Clarence said.

"I'm quite in earnest, Clarence. Without that helmet, do you think you can escape tomorrow night?"

Clarence gave the question some thought and then nodded his head. "If they don't put me in another helmet, I think I know a way out."

"Then we'll pray they won't have another helmet to put you in. One way or another, we'll know when we go back," Uncle Andrew said. "Now, let's go look at some birds."

We walked through the woods and fields of Mr. Mason's land, and I was surprised to find that Clarence really did know a lot about the birds we found. He even taught Uncle Andrew a couple of things. I tried to make notes about the birds so I could answer intelligently if anyone asked me. Eventually, I gave up. Once we got beyond blackbirds, sparrows, and mockingbirds, the names got too hard. They were called things like phoebe and nuthatch and waxwing and titmouse. Even now, I'm not sure I'm getting them right.

When it was time to go back to the plantation, Uncle Andrew reminded Clarence about running away the next night, then said, "Whatever happens, let's decide now that our rendezvous point will be north—at the hollow tree by Griffith's Creek. A friend told me about it. It's about 20 miles. Do you know where that is?"

"I reckon if I head north along Griffith's Creek, I'll find it," Clarence answered.

"Good man. So, by the grace of God, we'll be on our way within the next 48 hours. Can you hold on until then?"

"I'll try. I've waited this long, I think I can wait another 48 hours. Just so you promise we won't go without my little girl. 'Cause I won't."

"I promise."

Clarence suddenly stopped and grabbed Uncle Andrew's hand. "Thank you, sir," he said with tears in his eyes.

Uncle Andrew gazed into his face, then simply said, "You're welcome."

Back at the plantation, Hickocks started sputtering and went red-faced with the news that we didn't have the helmet. "You say you *lost* it?"

"Yes," Uncle Andrew answered. "I'm so sorry. It was scaring the birds, so we took it off in the woods and moved on. For the life of me, I couldn't remember where we put it. Neither could Jack or your slave."

Hickocks took a deep breath as he looked at us warily. "I

have no doubt that they couldn't! The master'll be upset."

"I'll be happy to make full restitution for the item," Uncle Andrew said.

Hickocks glared at him. "Full restitution? You think you can just walk into a store and buy one of those things? I made it myself. It was the only one we have."

I was relieved to hear the news. That would make our escape plan a little easier.

"Please, just name the price and I'll pay it," Uncle Andrew said in a voice that was full of mock regret.

"It's not for me to say," Hickocks snapped. "Take it up with Mr. Mason."

"I will. Wait here, Jack." Uncle Andrew strolled off toward the house.

Hickocks eyed me, then Clarence. "I don't know what you're up to, but I don't like it. I don't like it one bit."

"Up to, sir?" I asked.

"I won't be made a fool," he said, then looked steely-eyed at Clarence. "Listen to me, boy. If you run away again, you better make sure you're never found—'cause I'll kill you if I catch you. You hear me? I'll kill you."

"Yes, sir," Clarence said.

It scared me to hear Hickocks talk like that, and I was glad to hear Uncle Andrew and Mr. Mason return. Uncle Andrew must've charmed Mr. Mason again, because Mr. Mason didn't seem bothered about losing the helmet and insisted that his driver take us back to town.

At the carriage, Uncle Andrew told Mr. Mason that this

was good-bye.

Mr. Mason was surprised. "I'm sorry to see you go so soon," he said sincerely.

"We won't be too far away," Uncle Andrew replied. "I want to go to Colonel Ross's plantation first thing in the morning. I was told he has several species of woodpeckers on his property."

"Does he? How unusual. Several species? How marvelous for him. I never heard that."

"Perhaps I've got it wrong, but it will be worth investigating."

They shook hands, and then Mr. Mason signaled the driver to go. I glanced back, and it looked as if Mr. Mason was still pondering how Colonel Ross was lucky enough to have so many woodpeckers to look at.

I quietly asked Uncle Andrew about the lies he kept telling.

He looked at me as if I'd shocked him. "Lies?" he replied.

"You said you heard that Colonel Ross has woodpeckers. You didn't really hear that, did you?"

"I *said* I might have heard wrong," he explained.

"You know what I mean," I persisted. "You also said we lost the helmet. Isn't it wrong to lie like that?"

Uncle Andrew looked at me with a serious expression, his eyebrows pushed together in a thoughtful frown. "Jack, I've asked myself that question time and time again. Is it wrong? Well, let me ask *you* a question. Was Rahab wrong?"

I thought about it, but I couldn't remember who Rahab was. I shrugged and said, "Rahab was in the Old Testament, right?"

He smiled sympathetically. "The story of Rahab is in Joshua, chapter 2. She hid a couple of Joshua's spies, then lied to her king's men to protect them. Was she wrong?"

"I don't know. Was she?"

"People have been debating that question for centuries," Uncle Andrew replied. "On one hand, she lied. On the other hand, she protected two of God's men. Do you remember what happened? God brought the walls of Jericho down for Joshua and the Israelites. Because of Rahab's faithfulness, she was saved by Joshua."

"So they rewarded her for lying?" I asked.

Uncle Andrew nodded. "It seems that way. And there's an even more interesting twist to the story."

"What?"

"Read Saint Matthew, chapter 1. Rahab was an ancestor of King David, and in turn she was related to Jesus Himself. The apostle Paul even considered her a hero of the faith for what she'd done. What do you make of that?"

I didn't know *what* to make of it. "Are you saying that lying is okay?"

"Not necessarily," he replied. "God prohibits 'bearing false witness,' which means lying about your neighbor to bring unjust punishment against him. Rahab did not lie in that sense. Likewise, I am not breaking a commandment by what I do. I say what I say not to bring harm to anyone or to bring personal gain to myself, but to free men from their bondage."

We rode on silently while I thought about it. I kept thinking about it all the way through dinner, bedtime, and breakfast the next morning. As we got ready to go to Colonel Ross's plantation, I told Uncle Andrew what I thought about his explanation.

"I'm still not so sure about it," I said.

He smiled and clapped me on the back. "I thought that's what you'd say."

I waited to see if he had another answer.

His smile faded, and he looked deep into my face. "Jack, may God judge me if I'm wrong. But I am willing to risk His wrath to set these slaves free."

CHAPTER FIVE

Matt tells about his confession.

Okay, I need to tell you right up front that it was hard working in Colonel Ross's house. Just in the couple of days I was there, I worked until every muscle in my body hurt. At night, when Jonah said I could go to bed, I barely had the energy to wash my face before I collapsed onto that straw mattress and snoozed away.

We—I mean, the house slaves—were the first ones up in the morning. And when I say morning, I mean *morning*— even before the sun came up. We had to milk the cows and get breakfast ready for the Colonel and his wife. There were logs to split and the house animals to be fed (except Scout— he only let Eveline feed him). Then we dug in the garden, swept the porches, set the dining room for the next meal, polished silver, and washed clothes—and I'm not talking about using a washing machine. We had to use a washboard in a tub, scrubbing and scrubbing until our hands were all pruny. I was exhausted. Eveline, Jonah, Lizzie, and the other house slaves acted as if there were nothing to it. If they were tired, they never let on, and they didn't complain.

Eveline amazed me. I don't know where she got all her energy. Only a couple of times did I see her standing still by the back door or a window, looking out with a sad expression. She was thinking about her dad, I knew.

The whole time I was working, I had to keep reminding myself that I was doing it so I could come up with a plan to help Eveline see her father again. That's why I came back. But I wasn't sure how to do it.

I also kept wondering where Jack was. Did The Imagination Station take him back to Reverend Andrew? If it did, why didn't he come to rescue us? Every time a wagon drove up or someone knocked on the door, I kept expecting it to be him and Reverend Andrew. But he didn't show up.

I imagined him hanging out with the white folks, eating a lot of good food and being able to do whatever he wanted. It didn't seem fair. It *wasn't* fair. Just because the color of our skin was different didn't make it right for him to be better off.

Jonah was friendly the whole time, teaching us what to do. And he told us over and over to thank God for having it so good. That was hard for me considering all the work we did, but he said it was a lot worse on the other plantations. "Colonel Ross is a good and kind man," Jonah insisted. "There's no better master in the area. He takes care of his slaves."

"But we're *still* slaves," I reminded him.

He simply wagged a finger at me and told me to watch my mouth. "It's going to get you in big trouble, you hear?"

I mumbled that what I said was still true.

"There's no other master who brings in a doctor for his slaves or puts them in such nice quarters. He never uses the whip unless somebody really deserves it, and he even tries to keep the families together. No other master does that. But he does."

I didn't say a word, but that last part he said about keeping families together gave me an idea.

After breakfast on the third morning (I think it was the third morning, but I lost count), Jonah was all upset because one of the field slaves had been disobedient about his work. I guess he pretended to be sick and then was found later behind one of the sheds, goofing off.

Kinsey, the overseer, brought the slave to the back door. "Jonah! I don't have time to deal with him," he said. "You know what to do."

"Yes, Master Kinsey," Jonah said in a shaky voice.

I found out later that one of the reasons the field slaves didn't like the house slaves was that the house slaves were sometimes told to whip the field slaves.

Jonah, who was carrying a tray of tea for the Colonel, pushed it into my hands. "Take this to the study," he ordered.

"Yes, sir."

As I turned to go, I heard Jonah stomp down the back stairs and say to the disobedient slave, "Why do you make me have to do this? You know I hate it. You know it makes me cry. Why can't you behave so I won't have to whip you, boy?"

I carried the heavy tray through the house and into Colonel Ross's study. He was leaning over some ledgers, concentrating hard. I put the tea next to him.

"Your tea, sir," I said.

I guess he was expecting the voice to belong to Jonah. It surprised him to hear mine. He looked up and smiled, and his teeth glistened through his mustache and chin beard. "Thanks, son," he answered.

I didn't move away as I was supposed to. I had something I wanted to say. But I was scared, and it took me a minute to get my nerves together. Outside, dark clouds rolled in. I heard some distant thunder.

"Is there something you want?" the Colonel asked.

I shuffled my feet a little. "Colonel—er, Master Ross? I was wondering if we could . . . uh, talk, just for a minute."

"Talk?"

"I mean, you seem like a nice guy, and I thought maybe I could be honest with you about something."

The Colonel leaned back from his desk to give me his full attention. "Honest? Honest about what?"

I fiddled with the buttons on my jacket and worked up my courage. "The truth is . . . I'm not a slave."

"Aren't you?"

"No, sir. I'm free. I've always been free. The slave traders grabbed me and made me come here and then sold me, even though I told them I was free." There. It was out. I waited to see what he'd do.

The Colonel hit his palms against the top of his desk. "No! The scoundrels! How could they do that to you?"

I relaxed. "I don't know, but they did. You believe me, don't you?"

"Of course I do." The Colonel was on his feet in an instant, and the size of him—he was *big*—made me a little nervous again. He rushed to the door and called out to whoever was in hearing distance, "I want Jonah in here right away!"

"Jonah?" I asked. "But he doesn't know anything about it."

The Colonel waved at me to stay put. "Listen, son, Jonah's going to help me get to the bottom of this. For one thing, I want him to call Kinsey in from the fields. Kinsey knows those slave traders. If there's something illegal going on, I want to hear about it. Now, tell me what happened."

I was so relieved that I told him just about everything—about Eveline, Clarence, Odyssey, and how the slave traders grabbed us and brought us south. I told him everything except the part about Jack and The Imagination Station, since I didn't want him to think I was completely crazy. By the time I finished, Jonah showed up at the study door.

"Yes, master?" he asked, his body still shaking from the whipping he had just given that field slave.

"Jonah," the Colonel said, "step forward, please."

Jonah did, until he was standing next to my chair. He looked down at me, and I could tell he was confused. He knew something was going on but couldn't figure out what it was.

The Colonel sat down behind his desk again. "I want you

to take this boy and teach him a thing or two about lying."

"Lying!" I cried out.

Jonah grabbed me by the shirt and said sadly, "I knew it. It was just a matter of time."

"But—" I tried to get out words of protest, but nothing came.

"And boy," the Colonel said, "I suggest you keep your mouth shut in the future. Nobody here likes to think our fellow southern gentlemen are cheats."

"Come on, son," Jonah said and yanked me out of the room and through the house.

"No! No!" I cried the whole way. I squirmed, but Jonah's grip was like a vise.

"I told you, boy. I told you to keep your mouth shut. Now look what you've gone and done. I get done with one, and now I have to deal with another."

Going through the kitchen, I saw Eveline rush forward to help me, but Jonah stopped her. "Nothing you can do, child," he said. "There's nothing you can do."

He dragged me down the back stairs to the same spot where he had whipped the field slave. Drops of sweat still spotted the dirt under our feet.

"No, Jonah, don't," I pleaded. "I'm sorry. I was trying to help!"

He tied my hands to the hitching post. He sounded as if he was going to cry as he said, "I warned you, son. I warned you."

He picked up a long, slender switch. Thunder rolled above, and rain started to fall.

CHAPTER SIX

Jack tells about their arrival.

Uncle Andrew and I got to Colonel Ross's plantation late in the morning. The carriage pulled up the drive as the rain stopped. We climbed out, and Uncle Andrew gave the driver instructions to take our belongings to an inn about a quarter of a mile up the road. As we walked to the stairs leading to the door, we passed a puddle of mud. I glanced down at it, trying to be careful not to step in, when Uncle Andrew gave me a slight nudge. It was just enough to knock me off balance, and I fell to my knees—right in the mud.

"Hey!" I called out. "Why'd you do that?"

"You'll see," Uncle Andrew said.

The front door opened, and a wiry, old servant with a worried look greeted us. We stepped into the front hallway as Uncle Andrew introduced himself. The servant's eye fell to the mud all over my pants, then rose back to Uncle Andrew.

"I'll announce your arrival to the Colonel," he said before he shuffled off.

Colonel Ross came down the hall, and I was surprised by how big he was. He wasn't heavy, just tall. And he had long, curly hair, a mustache, and one of those little beards that stuck out from his chin. "The ornithologist!" he said. "I heard you were in the area. It's a pleasure to meet you. I'm Alexander Ross."

"This is my nephew Jack," Uncle Andrew said.

"An honor, Jack," the Colonel said, then looked down at the mud on my pants. "Did you have an accident?"

"Well, I—"

"Yes," Uncle Andrew cut in. "He tripped as we approached the porch. Would you mind if—"

"Jonah, take the young master here to the kitchen to see if you can wipe the mud off," Colonel Ross said.

"Yes, sir," Jonah replied and signaled for me to follow him.

The Colonel invited Uncle Andrew into the family room, while we walked in the opposite direction down the hall.

In the kitchen, a black woman with a scarf on her head was busy getting lunch ready. She hardly looked at me. The servant named Jonah led me to a large tub of water, grabbed a rag, and knelt down to wipe at the mud on my pants and shoes.

"I'll do it," I said.

"No, sir. I'll do it."

It didn't take long for me to realize that Uncle Andrew knocked me in the mud so I could have a look at the servants' areas. If Matt and Eveline really were here, I'd probably see them in the back. I also remembered that the slave trader told Uncle Andrew that Matt and Eveline had been sold specifically as house slaves.

"Don't dillydally, girl," the woman in the scarf said.

I looked up to see who she was talking to. I was surprised and happy to see Eveline standing at the other end of the kitchen. She just stared at me, her mouth hanging open.

I wanted to say something to her—hello and "Where's Matt?" and other things I was busting to ask—but she shook her head quickly.

"Go on, girl," the woman said.

Eveline walked past me and out the back door.

"Unless you want me to wash your britches, that's the best I can do," the servant said.

I looked down and saw that Jonah had gotten rid of most of the mud. "I think that's good," I said. "Thanks."

Jonah took me back to the family room. I got the impression that Uncle Andrew and Colonel Ross had become fast friends. They talked like old buddies. The Colonel insisted we have dinner with him, then apologized that his wife couldn't join us since she'd gone to visit her mother in Savannah.

"I don't know much about birds," the Colonel said, "but you're welcome to any resource I have that will assist your expedition."

"I'm obliged, sir," Uncle Andrew said, then hesitated as if he were about to ask the unaskable.

Colonel Ross picked up the hint. "You have a question, sir?"

"Mr. Mason was very kind to lend me one of his slaves. Jack is capable, but he's—"

"Say no more," Colonel Ross said. "I can certainly provide you with a slave."

"I saw one in the kitchen that would be perfect," I jumped in.

Uncle Andrew shot a heedful look my way. "Did you?"

"It's a young girl. I think she's just the right size to climb trees and find the nests."

Colonel Ross tugged at his whiskers. "There are better and more experienced slaves to send with you. The girl is new, and I'm not entirely sure I can trust her in an open field."

"I would take full responsibility, of course."

"I have no doubt that you would," the Colonel replied. "But taking responsibility isn't the point. I believe it would be reckless to send her with you. I'll send Washington instead."

****

Washington was a field slave who was probably in his thirties, but he looked as if he were my age. He talked more than any other slave I'd met—about his wife and children, the weather, the landscape, where we were from, birds—and I wondered if there was anything he *wouldn't* talk about.

I tuned out. My mind was on other things. I felt worried and discouraged that Washington went with us instead of Eveline or Matt. What were we going to do now? How would we contact them to say we were all going to escape that night? Where was Matt, anyway?

The dark clouds hung over us all afternoon. Uncle Andrew was real sneaky in how he asked Washington questions about his life as a slave and if he'd ever thought about escaping. Just then, Washington brought up the Underground Railroad.

"Yes, sir, I heard tell of a railroad for slaves. But I thought somebody made it up. Do you know anything about it, sir?" Washington asked.

I waited for Uncle Andrew to tell him the truth.

Instead, Uncle Andrew just shrugged. "Not much," he said. "Perhaps less than you do."

Rain spat down at us in small sprinkles, and we decided to go back to the Colonel's. After we made sure Washington was back in his slave quarters, I had a question for Uncle Andrew: "Why didn't you tell him about the Underground Railroad?"

"Didn't you notice how much he talked?"

"How could I *not* notice?" I snorted.

"If he talks that much about nothing in particular, how much more would he have to say about something really important—like us or the Railroad?"

"You mean he might be like a spy or an informer?"

"Possibly," Uncle Andrew replied. "There was something about the way he asked if I knew anything about the Railroad. He was too aggressive, particularly when you consider that I'm a complete stranger. How did he know I wouldn't turn the tables on him and report him to the overseer? So, if he isn't some sort of informer, he's reckless, which can be just as bad."

We walked along quietly for a minute, then I asked, "What are we going to do, Uncle Andrew? I've seen Eveline, but I don't know where Matt is. How can we find them and talk to them without making everybody suspicious? Do you want to throw me in another mud puddle?"

Uncle Andrew chuckled, then looked down at our clothes. We were covered with mud and leaves. "I don't think that will be necessary. Let's simply walk to the back door of the main house and ask to be cleaned off. Chances are we'll see Eveline and Matt in the kitchen, preparing for the evening meal."

I didn't realize how cold it was outside until we stepped into the warmth of the kitchen. The woman in the scarf was there, wrestling with a large duck. Eveline was there, too, peeling potatoes. She looked up at us but didn't react.

Uncle Andrew approached the woman with the scarf. "What's your name, my good woman?" he asked.

"I'm Lizzie," she answered.

"Lizzie, would you be so kind as to fetch us some fresh water so we can get the mud and leaves off our clothes?"

Lizzie looked down at her duck as if to say, "Can't you see I'm busy?" But Uncle Andrew kept his eyes on her, and she gave a quick curtsy and dashed out the door.

When we were sure it was safe, Uncle Andrew spoke softly to Eveline. "We're going to run away tonight, Eveline."

"Run away!" she gasped.

"Yes. We're going to run away and meet with your father."

Eveline's eyes went wide as dinner plates. "My daddy?"

Uncle Andrew nodded. "Now, how can we tell Matt?"

"Yeah," I asked, "where is he?"

Eveline's face fell. "Oh, no . . . no . . . we can't run away tonight."

"Why not?" Uncle Andrew asked.

Eveline looked around nervously, then wiggled a finger at us. "Come here."

We followed her up a small staircase to a room on the second floor. Eveline opened the creaky door. The room was dark. I could just barely make out the bed and the outline of someone in it.

"Matt?" Eveline whispered.

"Huh?" Matt answered weakly.

We moved closer to the bed. My heart pounded hard. I still couldn't see what was wrong with him, but I knew it wasn't good.

"Matt—it's me," I said.

"Hiya, Jack. Glad you could make it." Matt was lying on his stomach.

"What's wrong with you? Are you sick?" I asked.

"Yeah, kinda."

Eveline whispered, "Jonah took a switch and whipped him. I don't know why."

"I talked too much," Matt groaned. "Colonel Ross made him do it."

Uncle Andrew lifted the blanket and winced as he looked at Matt's back. He gently put the blanket down before I could see.

"Are you all right?" I asked. I felt an angry burning in the pit of my stomach. How could Colonel Ross do this to Matt? What kind of man beats kids like that?

"It hurts, but Eveline keeps putting some kinda lotion on my back."

"Jonah gave it to me," Eveline explained.

I leaned close and whispered, "Matt, if you're hurt, I have to call for Mr. Whittaker. We have to get out of here."

"No," Matt said weakly. "I said I want to finish this, and I will."

"Then you have to hurry up and get better," I said louder. "We're gonna run away tonight!"

Eveline pushed her knuckles against her mouth as if it would keep her from crying. "But don't you see? We can't!" she insisted. "Matt can't go anywhere. Not like this."

Uncle Andrew lowered his head, and for a second, I thought he was going to pray. "I'm afraid you're right, Eveline," he said. "We can't go anywhere tonight."

I looked at Uncle Andrew bug-eyed. "But Clarence is going to—"

"My daddy? You've seen my daddy?"

"Yes, Eveline. He's well. But we have a problem. Your father is going to try to run away tonight—and we won't be with him!"

CHAPTER SEVEN

Jack tells about the long night.

Why can't I run back to Mr. Mason's to warn Clarence?" I asked after we left Matt to sleep in his room.

"It's too far to run and would draw suspicion," Uncle Andrew answered as we walked down the stairs. "We can only hope that if he does run tonight, he'll simply hide and wait for us at the hollow tree."

Lizzie was in the kitchen with our tub of water. She gave us an uneasy look as we came down the stairs from the servants' quarters, but she didn't say anything except, "Your water is ready, sir. If you'll come over here, I'll clean off your trousers. Eveline, give us a hand."

I felt bad for Eveline. Watching her while she cleaned our pants and shoes, I kept thinking about her daddy and what he was about to do. What would he think when he got to the hollow tree and we weren't there?

Uncle Andrew and I sat down at the dinner table with Colonel Ross, and all I could think about was that he had ordered Matt to be beaten. I didn't know why. I didn't care. There was no excuse for it. I had to bite my tongue, because I wanted to say something nasty to him.

Uncle Andrew was friendly and nice to Colonel Ross. I figured he must be the world's greatest actor. He asked the Colonel about the local economy, the future of the South, and good investment practices.

Then dinner was served, and I felt bad all over again. Jonah brought in a large tray with the main course plates, and, seconds later, Eveline and Matt came in to serve the dinner rolls and gravy. Matt looked terrible and walked as if every move he made hurt him a lot. He wouldn't look me in the eye.

I wanted to jump on the table and ask the Colonel just who in the world he thought he was to have my best friend whipped! I know it wasn't very Christian of me, but I imagined what it'd be like to have the Colonel himself whipped.

The storm that had been hanging around all day suddenly broke right after dinner. The lightning flashed through all the windows, and the thunder shook the house. The rain fell in buckets.

"Where are you staying tonight?" Colonel Ross asked after we settled by the fire in the family room.

"I had our luggage sent to the inn down the road," Uncle Andrew answered.

"I won't have it," Colonel Ross said firmly. "You'll stay here tonight. I insist. I'll send Jonah to gather your things. I find you both good company and won't allow you to travel in such inclement weather. Jonah!"

****

I stood at the window and watched the rain fall against the glass. Uncle Andrew and Colonel Ross were playing chess at a small table on the other side of the room. The clock on the mantel chimed eight o'clock, and I wondered if Clarence had escaped yet. I had a tight feeling in my chest about it. It was awful, and the harder I tried not to think about Clarence running through the dark rain, the more I did.

"Sit down, Jack," Uncle Andrew said. "Read a book. You're making us both nervous standing there like that."

Colonel Ross agreed, "It's as if you're waiting for some bad news. You aren't, are you?"

"No, sir," I replied. "I'm just waiting for Jonah to come back with our suitcases."

Both of them looked at me as if I'd said a foreign word. It wasn't until later I learned that *suitcase* wasn't a normal word then. They used words like *trunks* or *baggage* or *luggage* instead.

A carriage raced up the driveway to the front porch and then stopped. I watched as Jonah leapt out and, along with the driver, started carrying our *trunks* up to the front door. The rain lashed at them as they did. The front door opened with a bang. Colonel Ross went to Jonah and barked instructions about where to put our belongings.

I think Jonah signaled the Colonel to come into the hall, because the Colonel said, "What? What is it?" and stepped out.

Uncle Andrew stood up at the table, and we both found ourselves drifting toward the door so we could hear better.

The Colonel caught sight of us and waved for us to come out. "One of Mr. Mason's slaves ran away," he reported. "Jonah heard about it at the inn."

My heart jumped into my throat.

"Truly? How did it happen?" Uncle Andrew asked coolly.

Jonah, still standing there dripping wet, explained, "It was one of Master Mason's new slaves. I guess he's run away before, so they fixed an ornament of some bells to his head to keep him from running away again. Now, I don't know how, but the ornament came off in the woods behind Master Mason's land, so Master Hickocks, the overseer, got his tracking dogs and found it hidden under some leaves."

I tried to keep from looking at Uncle Andrew. I suspected we were thinking the same thing: We should have *buried* that helmet.

Jonah continued, "Master Hickocks took the ornament back to the slave and said he was going to fix it on his head good and tight. Then suddenly, the slave acted like a madman and attacked Master Hickocks until he was barely conscious and then ran away into the fields. They're looking for him now."

"Pity the poor creature. If they catch him, they'll kill him," Colonel Ross said, then clapped his hands together. "Shall we finish that game of chess, Andrew?"

****

I was in my room, getting ready for bed, when I heard a knock at my door. I opened it, and Matt pushed past me with an armload of wood. "This is for your fire," he said, then dumped the logs next to the stove in the corner.

"Matt!" I said and closed the door fast. "Are you all right?"

"My back still hurts, but I feel okay." He sat down where he was and slumped wearily. "Did you hear about Clarence?"

I nodded.

"It's all the slaves downstairs are talking about," he said.

"How's Eveline? Is she upset?" I asked.

"What do *you* think? How would you feel if *your* dad was being hunted like some kind of wild animal in the woods?"

"Okay, it was a stupid question."

We looked at each other for a minute. The rain had stopped, and outside we could hear dogs barking somewhere far away. Were they chasing Clarence?

It was the unspoken question between us.

"What are we going to do?" Matt asked. "Does Reverend Andrew have a plan?"

"Sort of," I answered. "But we'll have to let you know what it is."

"Terrific," Matt said as if he didn't believe a word of it. He stood up to go. "I'm not going to fix your fire. You can figure out how to do that yourself."

"Do *you* want to stay in here tonight? You can sleep in my bed," I offered.

Matt looked at the big, cozy bed, and for a second, I could tell that's what he wanted to do more than anything. But he shook his head no. "It'll get us in trouble."

When he reached the door, I said, "Matt, we can stop this story right now if you want to."

"Do you want to?" he asked.

"You're the one who's getting hurt," I said. "It's up to you."

He thought about it a moment. "I said I was going to finish this story, and I am. If I go back now, I'll feel like a coward."

He slipped out the door and closed it quietly behind him.

I crawled into bed and wondered if I'd do the same thing in his place.

CHAPTER EIGHT

Jack tells about getting caught.

Morning came, and the clouds went. The sun shone through my window bright and warm. My first thought was that it was a good day for an escape. My second thought was of whether Clarence was caught or not. I prayed he wasn't.

I got dressed and went to Uncle Andrew's room just as he was coming out into the hall. "Good morning," he said without a lot of cheer. I guessed he was worried about Clarence, too. "Did you sleep well?"

"I slept okay," I said. "How about you?"

His voice went low. "Not well at all. I thought about Clarence mostly. Today we *must* work out an escape plan with Matt and Eveline."

Jonah appeared at the head of the stairs and said breakfast was being served in the dining room.

Colonel Ross was eating toast and sipping at his coffee when we walked in. He stood up until we were seated, then called for our food to be served. Matt and Eveline brought in plates of eggs, ham, and bread. We exchanged cautious glances. The Colonel said he had heard that the runaway slave from the night before hadn't been found yet.

"It's a nuisance," he said. "I can't imagine what goes through a slave's head. He has a place to live, steady work, food, and clothing. Why would he want to run away?"

I clenched my teeth to keep back what I wanted to say.

"Forgive me for saying so, Colonel," Uncle Andrew began, "but I believe that, for most of them, being a *slave* is cause enough to run away. I doubt that we as whites can appreciate what it is like to have one's freedom completely stripped away, but if we could imagine it, we wouldn't sit for it for very long. After all, what was your War of Independence for if not to be free from the rule of someone else?"

Colonel Ross gazed at Uncle Andrew. "By heavens," he said, "you almost sound like one of those abolitionists!"

Uncle Andrew chuckled as if the idea couldn't be more ridiculous. "I'm not a politician, sir, nor particularly active in your country's social issues," he said. "Would it be right for me, a foreigner, to intrude?"

"To be quite frank, I don't think it's right for *anyone* to intrude on the rights of a man and what he does with his possessions. You would no more want me to tell you what to do with the drawings you made of our birds than I would want you to tell me what to do with my horses, cattle, or slaves. Property is property, no matter how large or small."

I gripped my knife and fork until my knuckles turned white.

"To play the devil's advocate," Uncle Andrew replied, "we must remember that, in the case of slaves, we are talking about fellow human beings."

"Are we? I thought we were talking about *property*. And I will do with my property whatever I like, regardless of what those blasted abolitionists say."

I think it was probably because of the stress of the past couple days, but Uncle Andrew went red in the face and looked as if he wanted to say a lot of things to set the Colonel straight. Instead, he choked it all back. I mean, he *really* choked it all back—and started gasping.

The Colonel was on his feet right away and began pounding on Uncle Andrew's back. Finally, Uncle Andrew wheezed and got his breath back.

"Are you well, sir?" the Colonel asked.

Uncle Andrew nodded. "I'm so sorry. I simply found that hard to swallow."

"I suppose we've said enough about slavery," the Colonel said, then turned his head and raised his voice. "Have you heard enough?"

The doors to the dining room were thrown open, and several men—including Mr. Mason—marched in and surrounded the table.

"I certainly have!" Mr. Mason said in a loud and

excited voice.

"What is this?" Uncle Andrew asked.

Two of the men grabbed him, and one put a heavy hand on my shoulder. "Hey!" I cried out.

Mr. Mason pointed at Uncle Andrew. "There he is. Arrest him!"

Another man with wild, white hair stepped forward with a pair of iron handcuffs to put on Uncle Andrew's wrists. "You, sir, are my prisoner," he said.

"I demand to know the meaning of these actions!" Uncle Andrew shouted.

Mr. Mason leaned on clenched fists and declared, "I charge you with being an abolitionist!"

"What?"

"You persuaded my slave to run away!" Mr. Mason said. "If I had any doubt before, your words just now proved it!"

The two men holding Uncle Andrew yanked him to his feet. The white-haired man—who I guessed was a sheriff— put the handcuffs on him. "Let's go," he ordered.

"Go where?" Uncle Andrew asked. "Am I supposed to believe you're taking me to jail somewhere? This is a well-dressed lynch mob."

"Close your mouth, slave-lover," Mr. Mason said.

"Will you act the part of cowards by murdering me, or will you be brave and grant me a fair trial for these accusations?"

"Bring him!" Mr. Mason snarled.

Colonel Ross suddenly moved forward. "No," he said, "this

man will not be taken from my house unless I have your word that he'll be given a fair trial. I won't be party to a lynching!"

Mr. Mason glared at the Colonel. "Are you taking the side of this man?"

"I'm taking the side of justice, sir," the Colonel answered. "If you have an accusation, take it before our magistrate in Huntsville. Otherwise, leave now."

Mr. Mason snorted, then waved for the men to bring Uncle Andrew. "We will take him to the jail, on my word."

Colonel Ross stepped back.

"What about the boy?" the man with the heavy hand asked.

"Bring him along. He's probably an accomplice—or he'll make a good witness."

Mr. Mason and his men took us out to their wagon. As we pulled away, I saw Matt and Eveline watching us anxiously from the back of the house.

CHAPTER NINE

Jack tells about their day in court.

U ncle Andrew and I were taken to the Huntsville jail and spent the rest of the day and that night in a cold and damp cell. The guards were polite but didn't trust us. "You abolitionists are the curse of mankind," one of them said.

They asked us if we wanted to secure a defense lawyer.

Uncle Andrew chuckled and said, "Is there a lawyer in this town who would try to defend accused abolitionists? It's doubtful. I'll defend myself."

I spent most of the time worrying while Uncle Andrew read, prayed, and wrote in a diary.

"Aren't you afraid?" I asked at one point.

"Of course," he replied calmly. "But there's little sense in worrying about it. The outcome to this situation is entirely in God's hands."

I shivered most of the night, though I can't say whether it was because I was cold or scared.

The next morning, we were taken to a crowded courtroom. "We must be quite a sensation," Uncle Andrew said as we sat down.

Judge Thadeus Stallcup sat behind a tall, wooden desk and wearily asked Mr. Mason what the charge was.

"This scoundrel is an abolitionist who enticed my poor, weak-minded slave to run away," Mr. Mason said. "The slave attacked my overseer, dashed into the cold, wet night, and has yet to be found. I have no doubt that this man will bear the brunt of the guilt if anything tragic happens to that unfortunate slave."

"Mr. Mason, you had better elaborate the circumstances of this accusation and why you believe this man to be an abolitionist," the judge said.

Mr. Mason paced around the court in a dramatic style. "I will make a statement and call witnesses who will support my claim."

"Proceed," the judge said.

Mr. Mason continued, "This man, who goes by the name of Andrew Ferguson, called at my residence recently and requested permission to roam over my plantation to do a study of the birds there. In good faith, I granted it to him. He then claimed that one of my slaves—the one I had recently purchased called Clarence—knew something about local birds. He asked if Clarence might accompany him on his expedition, providing we removed the means we had secured to prevent him from running away again."

"Your slave has a history of running away?" the judge asked.

Mr. Mason nodded. "Yes, sir. When he was owned by Mr. Ramsay, he ran away to the North, then was captured and returned."

"And by what means did you secure him?"

"A head ornament with bells on it," Mr. Mason replied.

The judge turned to Uncle Andrew. "Why did you want the head gear removed?" he asked.

"The bells made an awful noise, which I was certain would scare away the birds I had hoped to study," Uncle Andrew replied.

The judge made a note of it, then waved at Mr. Mason to go on.

"He promised to take full responsibility if anything happened," Mr. Mason said. "They returned that afternoon without the head ornament. Mr. Ferguson claimed they had taken it off and forgotten where they left it. I realize now that it was merely a ploy to assist my slave's escape."

"Why do you believe it was a ploy?" the judge asked.

"Because my overseer later used his tracking dogs to find the head ornament. It had been clumsily stashed beneath a pile of leaves in the woods."

"Clumsily stashed?"

"If they had simply forgotten it, it would have been sitting next to a tree or on a log. But to be pushed under a pile of leaves makes me believe it had been intentionally hidden. Who but my slave, Mr. Ferguson, or his young assistant would have done it?"

The judge conceded the point. "Any response, Mr. Ferguson?"

Uncle Andrew shook his head and said, "Your honor, I would have to be clairvoyant to know how the helmet wound up under the leaves. We had misplaced it, and, after searching and failing to find it, we returned to Mr. Mason's plantation. I offered to pay for the item, but he declined."

"Is that true?" the judge asked Mr. Mason.

Mr. Mason was momentarily flustered. "Yes, it's true," he finally said. "He cleverly offered. As a southern gentleman, I refused his money out of courtesy. I have no doubt that as an abolitionist, he has the financial backing of wealthy northerners to pay for incidentals like that helmet. Unfortunately, it was the only one of its kind in this district. My overseer constructed it himself."

The judge scratched his temple and said, "Let me understand, then, that Mr. Ferguson returned your slave to you, but without the helmet."

"Yes, sir," Mr. Mason answered.

"Then what happened?"

"As I said, the next day, my overseer took his tracking dogs into the woods and found the helmet. He returned to the plantation, whereupon he attempted to place it back on the head of my slave. But my slave refused, attacked my overseer, and ran away."

The judge thought for a moment, then said to Uncle Andrew, "Your response?"

Uncle Andrew stood up. "Your Honor," he said, "I'm a

stranger in these parts and must submit myself to the mercy of the court. The evidence against me is circumstantial at best. I admit to borrowing Mr. Mason's slave and removing the helmet for the reason I had stated, but I see no proof that I enticed the slave to run away. That he did so was unfortunate for Mr. Mason and his overseer, but I cannot connect the event to anything I did. Surely you must be wondering the same thing, Your Honor."

The judge agreed. "Mr. Mason, if you're to make a case against Mr. Ferguson, you must have more evidence to prove he was an abolitionist who enticed your slave."

I breathed a sigh of relief. I couldn't imagine that Mr. Mason could come up with anything else. I breathed too soon.

"I have other suspicious elements, Your Honor," Mr. Mason said.

"Speak, then."

"I recall that when Mr. Ferguson first arrived at my residence, he said nothing about a slave of mine knowing much about birds. But after seeing Clarence in the field, he returned to say that he needed Clarence's assistance the following day. How did Mr. Ferguson come by this knowledge that Clarence was experienced with birds?"

The judge tilted his head to Uncle Andrew. "Mr. Ferguson?"

Uncle Andrew frowned and said, "I'm sorry, Your Honor, but my travels put me in contact with a large number of people, slaves included. I cannot recall where I was told that Clarence knew about birds."

A murmur through the crowd told me that wasn't a good answer.

"Perhaps you heard it from the slave auctioneer," Mr. Mason offered.

"I beg your pardon?"

Mr. Mason looked to the judge and explained, "Your Honor, I have here a witness who will testify that Mr. Ferguson had inquired about Clarence and two other slaves prior to setting foot on my property. Perhaps this gentleman told him about Clarence's knowledge of birds."

"Bring him forward," the judge said.

A large, bearded man came up to the witness box, gave his oath to tell the truth, then sat down. I recognized him as the slave auctioneer that Uncle Andrew and I spoke to when we first got to Huntsville. He was named Peter Fields.

"Did Mr. Ferguson approach you after the last slave auction?" Mr. Mason asked the man.

"He did, indeed," Fields answered. "He wanted to know about the slave you keep calling Clarence—the one I sold to you, Mr. Mason. He also asked about Clarence's daughter and another boy I sold to Colonel Ross."

"Were you aware that Clarence was an expert in birds?" Mr. Mason asked.

"No."

Mr. Mason directed his comments to the judge. "Is this mere coincidence, then, that Mr. Ferguson came to my plantation and then went to the Colonel's? I believe he was trying to find Clarence with the intent of luring him away.

Perhaps he had the same intent with Clarence's daughter and the other slave."

"That's merely conjecture, Your Honor," Uncle Andrew said. "I told Mr. Mason that I was going to Colonel Ross's—"

Mr. Mason cut in: "Because you had heard that the Colonel had several rare birds there. Again, I must ask, who told you the Colonel had such birds? I've spoken with the Colonel, and he was not aware of having rare birds on his property."

Uncle Andrew stood again and said, "I must say once more that I can't remember who told me about the Colonel's rare birds."

The crowd muttered to themselves, and I heard one or two voices say that the abolitionist should be punished. I felt frozen with fear about what would happen.

"How convenient," Mr. Mason snarled. "I'd like to ask Colonel Ross to please come into the courtroom, along with my other witness."

A bailiff called out the door for Colonel Ross. He entered and had Matt and Eveline with him, dressed smartly as attendants for the occasion, and the field slave named Washington.

On the stand, Colonel Ross admitted he couldn't positively say Mr. Ferguson was an abolitionist—only that he was *not* sympathetic to slavery.

"Are there any rare birds on your property, Colonel?" Mr. Mason asked.

"None that I know of," he replied. "Come to think of it, I

don't remember Mr. Ferguson saying anything about rare birds, either."

The crowd mumbled once more, and I began to sweat. This wasn't looking good at all.

"You lent him one of your slaves, didn't you, Colonel?" the judge asked.

The Colonel said he did. "I brought the slave with me to testify."

"So the slave is still here—he didn't run away?" Uncle Andrew asked. "I must be a poor abolitionist, then."

Laughter rippled through the crowd.

"Bring the slave to the witness stand," the judge said.

Washington took the stand and, after he'd been sworn in, was asked by Mr. Mason if he had talked to Mr. Ferguson about anything in particular during their afternoon looking for birds.

"Yes, sir," Washington replied as he fixed his eyes on the hat in his lap.

"What did you talk about?" Mr. Mason asked.

"Me and Master Andrew talked about the Underground Railroad. I don't know why, but he started telling me about it."

"That's a lie!" I shouted, then immediately regretted it when all eyes fell on me.

"Is there something you want to say, young man?" the judge asked me.

"No, sir," I said and sunk down in my seat.

Uncle Andrew patted my arm. "Your Honor," he said, "I

believe this slave is confused. Our conversation was the other way around. *He* asked *me* about the Underground Railroad, and I told him as much as I knew—which, in fact, was nothing."

Washington shook his head slowly.

The judge leveled a gaze at Mr. Mason and warned, "Sir, I will not have a contest of the truth between a free white man and a slave. I believe I'll disregard this portion of your case."

Mr. Mason nodded, and the crowd seemed to agree.

"Do you have anything else?" the judge asked.

Mr. Mason said, "No, Your Honor. I think what I've presented speaks for itself. This gentleman has concocted a series of untruths for some diabolical purpose—and since my slave has run away, I can only conclude that he enticed him to do so. I demand that this court punish him as a Negro thief, if not as a scheming abolitionist."

The crowd shouted their agreement.

After the judge quieted them down, he pointed at Uncle Andrew and ordered, "Rise, sir, and give your defense before I render a judgment."

Uncle Andrew stood up again. I held my breath. Whatever he was going to say had better be really good.

"Your honor," he started respectfully, "the evidence is circumstantial, and if one wanted to interpret it as diabolical, one could do so. However, there was nothing diabolical in my activities. I can only submit myself to the mercy of the court and hope you will see that I am an innocent man."

The crowd called out for the liar to be hanged. Uncle

Andrew sat down and leaned over to me. "If he finds me guilty, run for your life," he whispered.

The judge cleared his throat and spoke carefully. "I wish I could believe in your innocence, Mr. Ferguson. But the evidence speaks otherwise. If your intent was not to promote the abolitionist cause or give assistance to the slave's escape, please tell me your true purpose here. Everything indicates it was *not* to study birds."

A pause fell on the crowd as they strained to hear Uncle Andrew's reply. But he didn't have a chance to give one. A commotion erupted in the back of the courtroom. I turned around to see what was going on and nearly fell out of my chair with surprise.

Clarence walked into the room.

CHAPTER TEN

Matt tells about the surprise witness.

At the back of the courtroom, I stood with my eyes wide open and my mouth hanging down. Clarence waited by the door for a moment, looking unsure about what to do. Then he saw Mr. Mason and rushed forward. The crowd parted for him and gaped in wonder as he fell at Mr. Mason's feet and said over and over, "I'm sorry, master. I'm sorry I ran away."

The judge looked as if he was going to burst a blood vessel. He called for order in the court and insisted that Clarence take the stand and tell us what he was doing there. Looking tired and confused, Clarence agreed and sat down in the witness chair.

"All right, boy, tell us where you've been," the judge said.

"Well, sir, I'm sorry, I'm so sorry—"

The judge snapped impatiently, "You're sorry—that

69

much we understand. Now tell us the rest."

Clarence swallowed hard, then began: "It's all my fault, sir. After Master Andrew here took off that terrible big head ornament with the bells—so we could look for birds like he wanted—I promised myself I never wanted that thing put back on my head. You don't know what it's like, sir, unless you had it on yourself. It must weigh almost 15 pounds, and my suffering was great. Not only did it make my head and neck ache something awful, but you can't even lie down to sleep. No, sir, I had to sleep crouching down like some kinda animal. And after it came off, I thought to myself that I was never gonna let it be put on again. Never again . . ." Clarence put his head down and started to cry.

Now, I have to say right here that I had talked to Clarence enough to know he was a pretty smart man. But the Clarence who spoke in that courtroom wasn't anything like the person I knew. His voice was thick and shaky, and after a minute, it dawned on me that he was playing the part of the "dumb slave."

"Get control of yourself, boy!" Mr. Mason growled. "Tell us what happened!"

Clarence wiped his nose with the side of his sleeve. "I tried to hide that hideous helmet in the woods. But later on, when Master Hickocks showed up with it, I was afraid. I knew he was going to put it back on my head, and it was more than I could stand. As he came near me, I felt a horrible, horrible panic deep inside my soul, and it was like I was taken over by a wild animal. That's what it was like, sir. I turned into a wild animal and knocked poor Master Hickocks down and ran for the woods. I didn't know what came over me, 'cept I couldn't bear the thought of carrying that contraption on my head again."

The crowd started mumbling to themselves. I couldn't figure out if they were sympathetic to Clarence's story or not.

"I hid in the woods until my senses came back to me," Clarence explained. "And I thought I had to go back, 'cause I didn't wanna be a runaway anymore. Mr. Mason's is a good place to work . . ."

With that, Mr. Mason sat up in his chair and nodded.

". . . so I thought that I would just turn around and go back. I'd beg for mercy and pray for forgiveness. That's what I was gonna do, too, but then I fell in a hole in the woods and hurt my ankle. The pain was so bad that I couldn't move, so I just waited in the woods until I could walk again."

"Why did you come to this court?" the judge asked. "Why didn't you go back to the plantation?"

"I was going to, but on the road, I heard it told that poor Master Andrew had been accused of helping me run away. I felt awful, terrible. So I said to myself that I would come straight here so Master Andrew wouldn't be punished because of me. Here I am, Mr. Mason, and I'm sorry, sir. I'm sorry right down to my bones. I won't ever do anything like it again. You can even put the bells back on my head. That's how bad I feel."

Mr. Mason waved his hand at Clarence as if he was saying that all was forgiven and he wouldn't put the helmet back on.

"Mr. Ferguson," the judge said, "considering this evidence, I order that you be released at once and please accept this court's apology for any inconvenience or slight of your character this case has caused."

Reverend Andrew stood up. "Thank you, Your Honor," he said. "I am grateful for your time and the fair manner in which you conducted this investigation."

"Case dismissed!" the judge shouted.

It's hard to describe the chaos of the courtroom then. The place erupted. Everyone crowded forward to shake Reverend Andrew's hand or commend Mr. Mason for getting his slave back. A lot of things happened at once. Everyone seemed amazed that it turned out the way it did. I glanced over at Jack, but I didn't dare yell or wave. (Not that I could have anyway, because my body was still bruised and my back burned from the switching I got.) Eveline and I had to stay still at Colonel Ross's side with serious expressions on our faces. I was pretty sure, though, that Jack knew I was happy for them—and I figured Eveline was probably bursting to see her dad.

Then I saw Reverend Andrew quickly brush past Jack and race to Mr. Mason on the other side of the room.

Mr. Mason was all smiles again and shook Reverend Andrew's hand. Everyone got quiet so they could hear what the two men would say to each other. "Mr. Ferguson, I'm sorry for misjudging you," Mr. Mason said. "I should have respected my first impression that you were a true gentleman."

"Think nothing of it, Mr. Mason," Reverend Andrew said.

"There must be something I can do to make it up to you," Mr. Mason said. "Will you dine with me this evening? Allow me hours of contrition for what I've done."

"I will be happy to dine with you, sir, but I ask one other favor."

"Name it," Mr. Mason said.

"I beg you not to punish Clarence for what he's done. He admits he was a fool and behaved abominably against you and your overseer. But, for my sake, please do not punish him."

Mr. Mason looked as if he might not agree, then nodded yes. "I won't punish him," he promised.

Reverend Andrew shook Clarence's hand, and they swapped an expression that made me realize how brave Clarence was to come back as he did. He had risked his life for Reverend Andrew and Jack. It'd be easy enough for Mr. Mason to go back on his word and punish Clarence hard for what he'd done. And I had no doubt that Mr. Hickocks, the overseer, would want a hand in that.

Somewhere in the confusion, Reverend Andrew leaned down and said something to Jack. Jack looked up at me as if he wanted to say something, but Colonel Ross signaled for us to follow him out of the courtroom. "Come on," he growled.

I reluctantly obeyed and slowly followed. I didn't want the Colonel to have the satisfaction of seeing I still hurt. When we got out to his carriage, another man shouted at the Colonel, and they walked off together to talk. Eveline and I waited. I knew what she was thinking: She wanted to run to her father. I figured it was all she could do to stand still and just wait the way she was supposed to.

Jack suddenly came rushing through the front door of the court building, then saw us and tried to act casual. I looked around to make sure we weren't being watched, then wiggled a finger for him to come over.

"That was a close call," he said.

"I was sweating bullets," I said. My eyes locked on Eveline's, and for the first time, I noticed she'd been crying.

"Are you okay?" I asked her.

"I wanted to be with my daddy," she said.

Jack double-checked to make sure no one was listening, then said quietly, "Maybe you can be with him *tonight*."

Her face lit up.

"What's the plan?" I asked.

Jack shrugged. "I don't know, but Uncle Andrew said to be ready tonight. Can you make it?"

I stood up straight as if to show him my back wasn't bothering me. "I'll make it. I'm all better."

He looked as if he didn't believe me.

Jonah suddenly rounded the corner of the carriage and frowned when he saw Jack. "Scoot, boy," he said. "You're nothing but trouble around here. Go about your business."

"Yes, sir," Jack said and walked away.

He glanced back at me and Eveline one last time. I smiled and mouthed the word *Tonight*.

CHAPTER ELEVEN

Jack tells about the plan to escape.

At the inn later that afternoon, Uncle Andrew and I packed up the last of our things. "I don't get it," I said. "Aren't we worse off than we were? How can we escape tonight?"

"Because after tonight, I don't believe Clarence will ever have a chance to escape again. Here's my idea: I will go to Mr. Mason's for dinner. After the meal, I will ask to see Clarence—to once again thank him for helping me today. I suspect that Mr. Mason won't put Clarence back in that atrocious head gear until he's certain I'm out of the area. After all, he promised he wouldn't punish the poor man."

I sat on the edge of the bed. "So you'll get Clarence and make a run for it after dinner?"

"Crudely put, but correct. I will make as if to leave right after I see Clarence, then circle around to his quarters and escape."

"What if Mr. Hickocks is there? What if they're keeping a close eye on him?"

Uncle Andrew looked at me impatiently. "I didn't say it was a *foolproof* plan. Many things could go wrong. But we must pray we'll overcome any and all obstacles."

I wished I had his confidence. "What about me?" I asked.

"I want you to run back to the Colonel's and help Matt and Eveline escape."

"Oh," I said. "Is that all? Just walk in and help them escape?"

Uncle Andrew chuckled. "I have a friend who will create a diversion to help you."

"You keep talking about a friend who's gotten you information and sets things up. Just who is this guy?" I asked.

"Jack, in times like these, you never know when or where a friend will turn up," he answered. "Just listen. Hide near the back door. When the diversion comes, take Matt and Eveline and run for the hollow tree."

I folded my arms skeptically. "I don't know where the hollow tree is."

Uncle Andrew grabbed a large sheet of paper from the dresser and spread it out on the bed. "Take a look at this map and you'll have all you need to know."

CHAPTER TWELVE

Matt tells about the escape.

I couldn't figure out how in the world Reverend Andrew and Jack were going to get us all away. After the big courtroom drama, we went back to Colonel Ross's plantation and got to work as usual. Jonah told me to polish the silver in the dining room—which is what I was doing when the thunder roared and another storm dropped gallons of rain on us. The rain kept on going into the early evening.

The sun went down, and Eveline and I kept looking at each other, wondering what was going to happen. It drove me crazy, waiting like that. To make matters worse, Jonah was in a bad mood and kept telling me to do things. I had a feeling it was connected to the courtroom somehow. After all the excitement there, he seemed angry.

At one point, Scout, who was leashed to his doghouse just outside the back door, started barking at something.

Jonah yelled at him to shut up.

I had never heard Jonah yell like that.

"Go get some more wood for the fire," he said. I had just finished sweeping the kitchen floor, while Lizzie had Eveline cutting up carrots for dinner.

I looked out the back door at the downpour and hesitated.

"I said to go get some more wood!" he said harshly.

"Yes, sir," I said and ran into the rain. Scout peeked his head out of the doghouse and snarled at me. I thought, *He's just waiting for the chance to bite me. I know it.* I ducked around the side of the shed to where we kept the split logs covered. Just as I reached down to grab an armload, someone grabbed me from behind.

I was afraid it was Kinsey. He seemed to enjoy picking on the slaves—especially the house slaves, because he thought we were spoiled and pampered. I jerked away and spun around to face Jack.

"What took you so long?" I asked.

"I've been busy," Jack said.

"Busy with what?" I teased.

"Busy waiting here in the rain for you to come out. I couldn't figure how to get your attention without everybody seeing me."

I smiled because he was soaked from head to toe, his dark hair matted against his face.

"What's so funny?" he asked.

I shook my head. "Nothing. What's the plan?"

"All I know is that a friend of Uncle Andrew's is going to

create a diversion so you and Eveline can run out here. Then the three of us'll hightail it into the woods."

"*That's* the plan?" I said. I couldn't believe it.

"What did you expect? A squadron of helicopters to fly in and get you?"

"But who's this friend?"

"I don't know. Hasn't anybody shown up?"

"No. It's just the usual people. Mr. Colonel's wife is supposed to come home from her trip tonight, but that's it."

Jack rubbed his chin. "Do you think she's the friend?"

"Beats me."

"Well, I'll wait out here. Hopefully whatever's gonna happen will happen *soon*. I'm getting cold."

"You could always crawl in with Scout," I suggested.

"The dog? Are you kidding? I thought he was going to take my leg off when I first got here." Jack looked at the stupid grin on my face. "What? What's so funny?"

"You are," I said. I'd never admit it out loud, but it was really good to see him.

"Matthew!" Jonah shouted from the back door. "Where are you, boy?"

I started grabbing up some logs. "I'd better get back inside. Stay dry."

Jack nodded and retreated to wherever he had been hiding behind the shed.

Back in the kitchen, Jonah frowned at me. "What did you do, get lost?" he asked.

"No, sir." I threw some of the logs into the stove, and as I did, I leaned over to Eveline and whispered, "Be ready to run."

"What'd you say?" Jonah asked from the other side of the kitchen. "What's this whispering?"

"Nothing, sir," I said. Suddenly I was worried that Jonah would figure out what was going on and try to stop us from escaping.

Colonel Ross walked into the kitchen and pointed a finger at Eveline. "You—I want you to go up and prepare my wife's bedroom for her arrival tonight," he ordered. "I want it clean as a whistle."

"Yes, sir," she said and curtsied.

He looked at me and said, "Boy, I want you to give my boots a good polish. They're in my wardrobe."

"Yes, sir," I said. My mind went wild with the problems the Colonel's work would cause. If Eveline was in one room and I was in another, how would we talk? If we were upstairs, would we hear the diversion—whatever it was—when it happened?

I was surprised when Jonah spoke up. "Colonel," he said, "it might be better to wait until we have dinner all fixed and ready."

Colonel Ross looked at Jonah impatiently. "Are you telling me you and Lizzie can't make dinner yourselves? You sure got the work done before we had this boy and girl. Are you getting lazy?"

"No, sir, Colonel," Jonah said.

"Then I expect the work to be done," the Colonel said. He turned on his heel and walked out.

Eveline and I looked worriedly at each other and slowly started to follow.

Just as we reached the door, Jonah put his hand on our shoulders and pulled us back. "Don't go," he said.

I looked at him, confused.

He gave a signal to Lizzie. She nodded and picked up a large bucket of fat.

"Ready?" he asked.

"I . . . I don't understand," I said.

"This is your way out," Jonah answered. "You two grab your coats and get ready to run."

"You mean, *you're* Reverend Andrew's friend?" I asked, shocked.

"*We* are," Lizzie said.

"I reckon you could call us the departure depot for the Underground Railroad," Jonah said. "Now get ready to run."

We grabbed our coats and bundled up as fast as we could.

"Jonah!" the Colonel shouted from down the hall. He was coming our way.

"Hurry!" Jonah whispered.

Eveline and I were as ready as we were going to be.

Jonah waved at Lizzie and said, "Go on, woman—watch yourself."

Lizzie tossed the fat on the fire. It spat, then roared at her in a burst of flame.

"Fire! Fire!" Jonah yelled as he pushed us out the back door. The rain was still falling. Scout leapt forward and ran at us until his rope yanked him back.

Jack rushed out from behind the shed. "Is that it?" he shouted.

"Let's go!" I yelled back. We ran straight for the field.

Kinsey rounded the corner of the house and ran right into us. "What's going on here?" he asked.

"There's a fire in the kitchen," I told him.

Kinsey looked at the flames rising in the kitchen window, then suddenly looked at Jack, me, and Eveline. "What are you doing out here? Where do you think you're going?"

The three of us were speechless.

"You three get over there by the door. You're going to help fight this fire," Kinsey said.

"Fight it yourself!" I said and threw myself into Kinsey to give him a push. He tumbled backward into a feeding trough that was filled with water. "Run!" I yelled.

We ran into the darkness of the field, our feet splashing through the puddles and mud.

I heard Kinsey shout and turned in time to see him scramble out of the trough. He grabbed Scout's collar and untied him. "Get 'em, Scout!" he yelled.

Scout tore after us.

I shrieked, "Faster!" and we all picked up speed.

Just as we reached the edge of the woods, Scout caught up with us. I was sure he was going to dive at one of us, teeth first. But suddenly Eveline turned around and pointed a finger at him. "No, Scout! No!" she ordered.

Scout stopped dead in his tracks and looked at her.

"Go home!" she said.

Scout looked as if he couldn't make up his mind, barking and growling at us.

"Go home!" Eveline said more firmly.

Scout then turned and halfheartedly made his way back toward the house. I was shocked and wanted to ask her how she made Scout obey her like that. But there wasn't time.

"Come on," Eveline said, and we followed her into the woods.

The rain fell hard as we ran and ran until we couldn't run anymore.

CHAPTER THIRTEEN

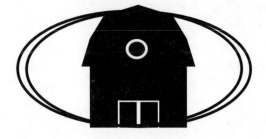

Matt tells about crossing the river.

Somehow in the storm, we found an old barn, where we hid under a moldy pile of hay. The next morning, we woke up huddled together, cold and hungry. The rain had stopped.

"We have to go," Eveline said as she stood up.

As far as I could tell, the sun was just peeking over the horizon. Jack refused to budge.

I tried to stretch out my stiff arms and legs. They hurt.

Eveline stood in the middle of the barn with a stern expression on her face and in her voice. "We have to go, y'hear?"

Somewhere in the silence of the morning, I heard dogs barking.

"Man, somebody owns a lot of dogs," Jack grumbled and rolled over.

"Those aren't dogs, they're hounds," Eveline said.

I sat up and looked at her to confirm what I thought she meant. "Hounds . . . that are hunting for us?"

She nodded.

"Jack!" I said and gave him a hard jab. "Those dogs want to have us for breakfast!"

Jack was on his feet before me and headed for the barn door. "We have to get out of here!" he said.

"And go where?" I asked.

Jack jerked out a crudely drawn map from his pocket and pointed to it. "We've been following Griffith's Creek all the way up. We need to get across and find the hollow tree."

"How many miles do you think we ran last night?" I asked.

Jack shrugged. "I'm no good at figuring that kind of thing. It felt like a hundred."

"I reckon we ran about 10 miles," Eveline said.

"Which means we have to run another 10," Jack said wearily.

"We won't be running anywhere if we don't get out of here *now*," Eveline said. "Those dogs are getting closer."

She was right. I could hear them barking and yelping. We checked to be sure there wasn't anyone around the barn, then made a mad dash for Griffith's Creek.

Though the rain had stopped, Griffith's Creek was flooded. It poured over both banks in a torrent.

"What do we do now?" I asked as I tried to figure our chances of crossing over.

Jack, panicked, pulled out the map again and looked for an alternate route.

"That won't help us," Eveline said. "We have to follow it north and hope to the Lord that we'll find a place to cross over."

Jack and I agreed with her and were just about to leave when a dog barked behind us. We nearly jumped out of our skins.

"Scout!" Eveline said.

I couldn't believe my own eyes. "Did he follow us?"

"Or maybe he's leading those hounds to us," Eveline said. "That's what he's trained to do."

Scout paced back and forth a few feet from us.

"Go home, Scout!" Eveline shouted. He didn't obey her.

"Well?" Jack asked. "I'm all out of doggie biscuits."

"Should we throw rocks at him?" I asked.

"No," Eveline said. "It'll only make him mad—maybe attack us himself."

"He likes you. He wouldn't attack . . . would he?" I wondered.

Eveline watched Scout, then reached out and took my hand. "Hold hands," she ordered.

"What?"

"Hold hands real tight. We have to go into the creek."

Jack hesitated. "But we don't know how deep it is," he complained.

"We can't stay here," Eveline said impatiently. "If we go in the creek, if we can make it across, the dogs'll lose our scent. Maybe even Scout won't follow us. He's not crazy enough to get in this water."

I protested, "If *he's* not that crazy, why should we be?"

"Because *he* won't get whipped and sold when they get him back to the plantation," Eveline answered.

The three of us grabbed hands and slowly waded into the cold, rushing water of Griffith's Creek. Scout whined at us from the creek's edge but didn't follow. In fact, he did something I never expected: He lay down and put his head between his two front paws.

"What's he doing?" I asked Eveline.

She glanced back. "I don't know," she said. "Funny, but if he's the lead dog of the pack, he should've run back to help guide the rest of the hounds to us."

The water was up to our waists, and we strained with all our might to hold on to each other. The current threatened to knock us over. One wrong step and I knew we'd be goners.

"This is no creek," Jack said, "it's a *river*."

The hounds were still in the distance but getting closer all the time. Scout stayed where he was along the creek's edge. I didn't know much about dogs, but what he was doing didn't make any sense.

Suddenly Eveline let out a shriek. "It's the lead hound!" she cried.

I looked over my shoulder and saw a single mangy-looking dog follow our scent to the creek. He seemed excited. Oblivious to Scout, who stayed put, the hound pranced back and forth, barking and howling. Even in that dim morning light, I saw his long, white teeth and the slobber that sprayed back and forth. I imagined a whole pack of them rushing into the water to make a meal out of us.

"What's that mean? There's only one," Jack said.

"The rest'll be here soon," Eveline said in a choked voice. "God have mercy!"

I didn't know which was worse, wading into that deep creek with the fear of falling and drowning, or facing the coming dogs.

It's hard to talk about what happened next because it was so horrible, but it saved our lives. Scout, who had been lying perfectly still, suddenly lunged out at the hound. I don't think it knew what hit it. In a flash, Scout had the hound's throat in his vicelike jaws. The hound yelped, but the sound was cut off instantly. It fought to get free, wrenching its head back and forth, but Scout wouldn't let go. Pretty soon, the hound's struggle ended, and it went limp.

We stood mesmerized where we were in the water, too terrified to make a move.

Scout shook the hound a couple of times and, sure that it was dead, dragged its carcass to the creek. The current caught the hound and sent it floating away downstream.

With tears running down her face, Eveline cried out, "Thank you, Scout! Thank you! Oh, thank You, Lord!"

"What happened?" I mumbled.

"The rest of the pack'll be lost without their lead hound," Eveline said. "Hurry! Move upstream!"

We got to shallower waters and waded against the

current and away from Scout. He didn't follow but stood watching us.

"Come on, Scout!" Eveline called.

We joined in. He was our hero now. We didn't want to go on without him.

Scout just watched us for a moment, then suddenly turned and ran away into the woods. I wanted to believe he was coming up with a scheme to lead the pack of hounds away from us. After what I had just seen, I could believe anything of that dog. The hounds' barking soon faded until we couldn't hear them anymore.

Staying in the creek, we waded about a quarter of a mile until we found a section with a fallen tree. It worked as a bridge for us to get across.

Safe and sound, Jack got a bright idea. "Let's try to knock the tree into the creek," he suggested. "Then it'll be even harder for anybody to follow us."

"What about my daddy and Reverend Andrew?" Eveline asked.

In our rush, I think I had it in my mind that they were already up ahead of us, waiting at the hollow tree. It hadn't occurred to me that they might still be somewhere behind us—*if* they had been able to escape at all.

Eveline's sad expression made me and Jack feel awful. We had forgotten, but she hadn't.

"How will they get across?" she asked.

"What if we're *already* across?" Clarence asked as he stepped out from behind a tree. He stretched out his arms toward his daughter.

"Daddy!" she shouted and ran into one of the best hugs I've ever seen in my life.

"Hello, my baby," Clarence said.

"Well, boys? How did you do?" Reverend Andrew asked. He stepped out from behind another tree nearby. "I was getting worried about you."

"Uncle Andrew," Jack said, relieved to see him. "You were worried about *us?* Nothing to it. We were getting worried about *you.*"

"It was a piece of cake for us—once I gave that overseer a good knock on the head," he replied.

"That makes two he's gotten in the last couple of days," Clarence said with a laugh.

"Why didn't you tell us Jonah was the friend you kept getting your information from?" Jack asked.

"Because I didn't dare risk that you could expose him. He and Lizzie are two of the most valuable assets we have in the Underground Railroad. They feed us helpful information constantly—and the Colonel would never guess it. You see, Jack, you never know when or where your friends will turn up."

I thought about Scout and figured that truer words had never been spoken.

CHAPTER FOURTEEN

Matt tells about their "ride" on the Underground Railroad.

Within a few hours after we were all together again, Reverend Andrew led us to the first "stop" on the Underground Railroad to the north. It was a farmhouse in the middle of nowhere. An old man and woman fixed us a hot meal and let us sleep in beds they'd set up in some secret rooms near the back of the house. When night came, we headed out again. We walked for miles and miles along dirt roads, through damp woods, and across muddy fields.

It was tiring, but just about the time we thought we couldn't walk anymore, we came to another "stop" and felt okay again. People all along the way greeted us like long-lost family. I knew then how it must have felt for blacks to go from the cruel treatment of the slave-owning whites to the kindness and generosity of those whites who wanted slavery abolished—and would sacrifice all they had to make it that way.

Jack and I talked about ending the adventure. Since Clarence and Eveline were back together, we thought we could tell Whit to flip the switch that would stop The Imagination Station. But we both had a nagging feeling the story couldn't really end until we were back where we started: in Odyssey.

There isn't much point in telling everything that happened on our journey. I guess it's enough to say that we made it back to Odyssey on a cold evening while the sun set over the town. We went straight to the church, where Reverend Andrew—even Jack started calling him "Reverend" again—said he would start a fire in the big potbelly stove and would make us rest on the beds in the basement. But we had forgotten that the basement was torn up when the slave hunters broke in. *It was such a long, long time ago,* I thought.

"Then we'll go to my hotel," Reverend Andrew said.

We all reacted the same way, and basically it came down to: "Are you nuts? Don't you remember what happened before?"

Reverend Andrew shook his head. "I remember well enough—and after what we've been through, I defy *anyone* to bother us now."

Clarence spoke up first. "With respect, Reverend, I think we'd all feel better if you were *sure* we could get to the hotel safely. Otherwise, I'm happy to stay here—or move on to the next station—as long as I'm with Eveline."

Reverend Andrew looked at them both, then agreed. "Jack, do you want to come with me?"

"I guess so," Jack answered.

"We'll be back in an hour," Reverend Andrew announced.

But things weren't right in Odyssey, and it was a lot less than an hour before we saw them again.

****

Jack picks up the story.

Reverend Andrew and I walked to the hotel just as the shops were closing the day's business. I wish I could describe the looks on people's faces when they saw us (well, not us really—Reverend Andrew mostly). You could hear the "buzz" of everyone talking.

We got to the hotel, and Reverend Andrew went straight up to the manager's office door and knocked hard.

"Come in," a voice called from the other side.

Reverend Andrew opened it, and a well-dressed man with slicked-down, brown hair and a handlebar mustache stood behind a big, oak desk. He couldn't hide his surprise. "Reverend! You're back!"

"I am, indeed, Nathaniel," Reverend Andrew said. "I went south to reclaim those poor souls who were taken from me."

"Come in, come in, sit down," Nathaniel offered.

Reverend Andrew declined. "I'll get to the point, my good friend. I have the three Negroes with me, and I want to bring them back to my rooms for a bath and a rest. Do you have any grievances with that?"

Nathaniel's eyes bugged out. "Now, Reverend, you know that I, personally, do not have a grievance against it, but you've been away for a while, and . . ." He signaled for us to come fully into his office, and after we did, he closed the door.

"This is a bad time, Reverend," he explained. "The town is torn apart by arguments between the abolitionists and the proslavery factions. Twice now we've had assemblies in the streets that I feared might lead to violence. If you brought your Negroes into the light of day—and to this hotel—I don't believe we'd survive it."

"Then so be it," Reverend Andrew said. "Perhaps it's time for Odyssey to make up its mind about what it believes."

Nathaniel's expression was calm, but his voice shook. "That may be true, but the law remains on the side of those who support slavery and the return of any runaway slaves. The slave hunters, those who caused all that trouble before, are here. You'll risk the lives of your friends by bringing them out into the open. The slave hunters will take them again."

"Perhaps it's time for Odyssey to force a change in the law. The slave owners are so adamant about states' rights, then what about *this* state's right to throw the slave hunters out on their ears?"

"I'm just a hotel manager," Nathaniel said as an appeal.

"And I'm just a pastor," Reverend Andrew said. "We all have a responsibility to our brothers in need."

Nathaniel frowned. "It's dangerous," he said.

"Most of the great causes are. Will you send one of your trusted staff to Adam Green's place? Please tell him I've returned and that I'm expecting trouble."

"Then?"

"He'll know what to do."

We walked back into the lobby, where the guests eyed us nervously. A short man with a twitchy face raced up to Reverend Andrew and whispered in his ear. Reverend Andrew nodded and thanked the man.

"I have a bad feeling about this," I said.

"So you should," Reverend Andrew said as he picked up his pace to a jog. "The slave hunters know we're here. We have to get back to the church immediately."

We got there in a few minutes, and we didn't like what we saw as we walked up to the door. Several men with torches sat on horseback. One climbed off, and I remembered from before that he was the sheriff. He had black and white stubble all over his face and looked tired. Though it was a cool evening, there were dark rings of sweat around his armpits.

"Good evening, Sheriff," Reverend Andrew said cordially.

"Reverend, I'm glad to see you back in town."

"Thank you. I appreciate you coming here personally to say so."

The sheriff scratched at his stubble. "I'm here to make sure we don't have any trouble," he said. "Have you got runaways in your church?"

"I have a free man, his daughter, and a freeborn boy visiting my church," Reverend Andrew explained.

The sheriff winced. "Aw, now, Reverend . . . why? Do you have any idea of the problems I've been having around here?"

"You have my sympathy," Reverend Andrew said with a smile. "Let's go inside, Jack," he told me. "We need to start that fire, make some tea, and fix up those beds."

He and I stepped toward the front door.

"Reverend—"

"Listen to me, Sheriff," Reverend Andrew said as he pushed open the door. "I don't want any trouble, but I have a feeling it's going to come anyway. I suppose you and your men should decide now on which side of the trouble you wish to place yourselves." With that, we walked inside, and he closed the door.

Just as Reverend Andrew had said, we built a fire in the big potbelly stove, made some tea, and fixed the beds in the basement. No one felt much like sleeping.

"What do you reckon will happen?" Clarence asked.

Reverend Andrew shook his head. "Only God knows, Clarence," he answered. "But my educated guess is that the slave hunters will come and try to take you back again."

"We won't go back," Clarence said firmly. "We'd rather die first."

Matt and I exchanged glances across the room. Was this part of the story? Were Clarence and Eveline really supposed to be hurt when they got back to Odyssey? Was our part in this whole thing just to bring them to their deaths?

A door slammed in the sanctuary upstairs, and Reverend Andrew excused himself to go investigate. I said I'd go with him, but he waved me back.

Eveline cupped her mug of tea in her hands and began to pray softly to herself.

Clarence leapt to his feet and declared, "No, sir, we haven't come all this way *again* just to get caught. No, sir. I won't let it happen."

I decided to creep upstairs to see what was going on.

"I'm coming with you," Matt said.

The front door of the church was open just a crack, and we watched while Reverend Andrew talked outside to two of the slave hunters who'd captured Clarence, Eveline, and Matt before. One was tall and had a hooked nose and bushy mustache. "That's Hank," Matt whispered.

The other man had a round baby face and wore a vest stretched tight over his big belly. Matt said his name was Sonny.

The two slave hunters were arguing with Reverend Andrew about handing over Clarence and Eveline. "We'll let you keep the one who says he's free," Hank said.

"Gentlemen," Reverend Andrew said, "my church is a sanctuary, and I warn you that if you enter it with the intention of capturing *anyone* inside, I will be forced to take action."

The sheriff stepped forward and said, "I believe there must be a peaceful solution to this conflict. I won't have violence in my town. I promise you, I won't."

"Then you'd better do something, Sheriff!" a man in the gathering crowd shouted. The light from a torch flickered on his face. I remembered him from before, too. He was a loudmouth who believed in slavery. "Some of us in town are getting sick of the way Reverend Andrew here ignores the laws! These men have a *right* to take those runaway slaves back to their masters!" The crowd shouted their agreement.

"Now hold on, hold on," the sheriff said.

Another man pushed to the front of the crowd and shook a fist in the loudmouth's face. "No one has the *right* to take another man as a slave!" he said. "And I'm telling all of you now, there are those of us in Odyssey who won't tolerate these slave hunters anymore!"

"There are those of us who won't tolerate you slave lovers anymore!"

The two men started pushing each other. The sheriff stepped in. "Stop it, boys!" he ordered.

They pushed him away. Then the crowd moved forward with shouts from both sides. Fists started flying. We stepped aside so that Reverend Andrew could back into the church and close the door. Then he locked it.

"Is that a riot?" I asked, wondering why I wasn't more afraid.

"I always knew it would come to this," he said sadly. "Citizen against citizen, brother fighting against brother.

That's what the cruelty of slavery does to men's hearts." Bodies banged against the door as the shouts continued. I thought I heard a gun go off.

Matt said, "Reverend Andrew, one of them's missing. I didn't see Boss."

"Boss?"

"He's the leader. Remember? There were *three* slave hunters. Why wasn't he out there?"

Just then we all got the same idea: "He's sneaking in through the tunnel!"

We ran back through the church and started down the wooden steps to the basement. Eveline was sitting on the edge of her bed. Clarence was using a poker to jab at the fire. Boss, a squinty-eyed man with thick eyebrows and a permanent frown on his hard face, was sneaking in through the tunnel door. He had a gun drawn.

First, Reverend Andrew shouted from the stairs, "Boss!"

Boss looked up, and Clarence, thinking fast, spun around with the poker and threw it at the slave hunter. Boss raised his arm and deflected the poker away onto one of the mattresses.

In that split second, Clarence leaped like a tiger onto Boss. They slammed against the wall, the gun waving around wildly in Boss's hand, and then they fell onto the mattress where the poker was. Clarence was on the bottom, and his back pressed against the hot spike. He screamed and threw Boss off. The gun slipped from Boss's hand and landed at Reverend Andrew's feet as he was rushing toward the two men.

Reverend Andrew snatched up the gun just as Boss grabbed the poker. Boss was about to hit Clarence with the poker when Reverend Andrew fired the gun. Boss grabbed his side as he spun around, then collapsed with a groan to the ground.

We stared at Reverend Andrew. I think he was as shocked as we were at what he'd done.

"Through the tunnel!" he shouted. "We have to get out of here!"

"What about me?" Boss cried out, still clutching his side.

"I'll come back for you, son," Reverend Andrew said as he picked up an oil lamp. "You deserve to be left here, but I'm a servant of God, and I'll come back. I promise."

We followed Reverend Andrew through the door into the dark tunnel. He lit the lamp. "This way," he said.

Somewhere, farther up the tunnel, we heard shouts. Boss must've heard the shouts, too, because he started calling for whoever it was to come help. "They're in here! Don't let them get away!"

"Where do we go now?" Clarence asked.

Reverend Andrew suddenly stopped midway up the tunnel and turned to the wall. "Push this," he told us. He pushed at the wall. The rocks gave way and spilled outward. We helped until we'd cleared the entrance to *another* tunnel. "It's my emergency escape," he said.

We ran down the tunnel, skipping over fallen rocks and coughing at the thick air.

"Are you sure this leads somewhere?" Clarence asked.

"To the old rectory," Reverend Andrew explained. "It's the ruined house not far away."

I remembered seeing it the first time we tried to escape from the church.

We reached the end of the tunnel and saw a wood ladder. "Hold this, please," Reverend Andrew said and passed the lamp to Clarence. He climbed up the ladder and pushed at something above. It sounded like a latch. With a rusty groan, it opened, and a burst of fresh air poured in. Scrambling up the ladder, he called for us to follow.

I nearly had a heart attack when we got to the top. We were in the middle of what looked like the remains of a house. A band of men with torches and horses surrounded us, and I thought for sure that we were caught.

"Thank you for coming, Adam," Reverend Andrew said to a man at the front of the group.

"Glad you're back, Reverend," Adam said. "What would you like me to do?"

Reverend Andrew gestured to us and said, "Take these friends of mine to the next station on the Railroad. They're not safe here."

"Yes, sir," Adam said. "Can you ride horses?" he asked us.

Clarence nodded and said, "I can. My daughter can ride with me."

"Then get on. I don't think it'll be long before that riot makes its way here."

We looked in the direction of the church. The shouts and chaos were unmistakable. It was a full-scale riot.

"Oh, no," Reverend Andrew said. Flames reflected off the glass on the inside of the church. "They're burning my church down!"

Clarence climbed on the horse and then pulled Eveline up to his lap.

"What about you two boys?" Adam asked.

"We're staying," Matt said.

Reverend Andrew turned to face us. "You can't," he said to Matt. "They'll try to take you as a slave again."

"They won't be able to," Matt said.

Reverend Andrew persisted, "I don't know that I can stop them."

"You won't have to stop them," I said with a strange confidence. "We have another way out."

"How?"

I smiled at him. "You never know when or where your friends will turn up."

Reverend Andrew turned to Adam and said, "Go, then. Hurry."

"Right," Adam said and gave his horse a nudge.

"No, wait," Clarence said. "Reverend . . . Matt . . . Jack . . . I don't know how to thank you." He reached down and shook our hands.

"Thank you," Eveline said. She had tears in her eyes. Suddenly, with Clarence holding on, she threw herself halfway off the horse and grabbed Matt to kiss him. She pulled me close, too, and kissed me on the cheek. Then Reverend Andrew.

"Lord love you," she whispered.

Clarence pulled her back up, tugged at the reins on his horse, and steered it away. Adam and his men followed. With a "Hyah!" command to their horses, they raced off into the night.

The mob around the front of the church drifted to the side, and someone saw us. With shouts and angry gestures, the crowd moved our way.

Reverend Andrew gestured to us and said, "Well, boys? Care to run for the woods?"

I looked at Matt, and we both knew it was time to go home.

"Good-bye, Reverend Andrew," I said. "Thank you for everything."

He shook my hand. "You're welcome, Jack," he told me. "You made a nice nephew for a while."

"See ya, Reverend Andrew," Matt said and held out his hand.

Reverend Andrew took it but pulled him close for a hug. He then wrapped his other arm around me.

My face was buried in his side so that all was dark. I felt that roller-coaster feeling again and thought my legs might slip out from under me.

I heard Matt say, "Hey, what's going on?"

And then The Imagination Station wound down.

CHAPTER FIFTEEN

Matt wraps it up.

The Imagination Station door *whooshed* open. Mr. Whittaker stood just outside, with his hands on his hips. "Well?" he asked.

Jack crawled out. "What an adventure!" he said.

I got out behind him and realized right away that I didn't feel stiff or sore. I reached up and touched my back where I'd been whipped. It felt fine. "That's weird. I wasn't hurt," I said.

"I hope not," Mr. Whittaker said with concern. "Whatever you experienced in The Imagination Station should never come out with you—except what you learned, of course."

"So . . . was it *all* just in our imaginations?" Jack asked.

"Yes . . . and no," Mr. Whittaker said with a smile. "The stories you went through are based on the truth, on history. It was your imaginations that let you take part in them."

"What happened after we left?" I asked. "What became of Reverend Andrew and Clarence and Eveline and—"

Mr. Whittaker held up his hand. "One thing at a time. Let's talk about Odyssey."

"Yeah, we left in the middle of a riot. I didn't know we had riots in Odyssey," Jack said.

Mr. Whittaker pointed to the old newspaper on the workbench. "The Odyssey Riots of November 1858 are well known to anyone who's studied our local history. They caused several things to happen—some good, some not so good. The town finally made up its mind about how it felt toward the slavery issue—and became the first in the state to refuse to cooperate with slave hunters."

"That's good," I said. "What's not so good?"

"The church burned down."

"No!" Jack cried out.

"Everything except for the church tower. It was the only thing left standing. You can still see it."

"Where?" I asked.

"Right upstairs," Mr. Whittaker answered. "It's the tower you see on the side of Whit's End."

"What?" Jack and I said together.

His white mustache spread out in a broad smile. "Uh huh. This building was built on the site of the church. The tunnel leading into this very workroom was used by Reverend Andrew and the Underground Railroad."

"What happened to Reverend Andrew?" Jack asked.

"Reverend Andrew Ferguson became a leading light in the fight against slavery. He later lost his life while ministering to Union soldiers during the Civil War."

This made Jack and I go quiet for a moment. I think we had hoped he lived on for years and years.

"It shouldn't surprise you that he would sacrifice himself that way," Mr. Whittaker observed. "He said he was God's servant, and he believed it through to death."

"How about Clarence and Eveline?" I asked.

Mr. Whittaker smiled again. "You'll like this part. Clarence and Eveline took the Underground Railroad all the way to Canada, where they were reunited with Lucy—Clarence's wife and Eveline's mother. They lived there until Clarence died, then Lucy and Eveline moved to Chicago. Eveline got married to a fine gentleman named William Teller, and they had children of their own."

I thought about it quietly for a minute and had a strange feeling. "Maybe one day we'll bump into someone who was related to them," I said. "Maybe they don't know all their ancestors went through to be free."

"Maybe so," Mr. Whittaker said. "But now you know, right? You've seen what it's like to be in a time when you couldn't take freedom for granted."

We nodded.

He continued, "I hope that makes you appreciate your freedom even more now—that it's something to be treasured."

As a kid who had never thought much about being black,

I realized I had a lot to be thankful for.

****

When I got home, I asked my mom and dad if we had any books or papers about the history of our family. They were surprised that I would ask, but they said they did. Dad took me into our little family library and pulled out a book with "Our Family Record" stamped in gold on the front.

"Because our ancestors were slaves, the records don't go back very far," my dad explained.

"How far back does it go?" I asked.

He pointed to the top of a page where a tree had names filled in on various branches. "Right there."

Clarence and Lucille, it said on one side.

He traced his finger down to the next line. *William & Eveline Teller.*

I followed the lines down the page until the names came to my grandfather, then my father and his family. "No way," I said in complete and absolute disbelief. "You mean, I'm related to Clarence and Eveline?"

Dad looked at me, puzzled. "Sure. Why? Do you know something about them?"

"Oh, Dad," I said with a laugh, "have I got a story for you!"

The End

Don't Miss a Single "Adventures in Odyssey" Novel!

Strange Journey Back

Mark Prescott hates being a newcomer in the small town of Odyssey. And he's not too thrilled about his only new friend being a girl. That is, until Patti tells him about a time machine at Whit's End called The Imagination Station. With hopes of using the machine to bring his separated parents together again, Mark learns a valuable lesson about friendship and responsibility.

High Flyer with a Flat Tire

Joe Devlin has accused Mark of slashing the tire on his new bike. Mark didn't do it, but how can he prove his innocence? Only by finding the real culprit! With the help of his wise friend Whit, Mark untangles the mystery and learns new lessons about friendship and family ties.

The Secret Cave of Robinwood

Mark promises his friend Patti he will never reveal the secret of her hidden cave. But when a gang Mark wants to join is looking for a new clubhouse, Mark thinks of the cave. Will he risk his friendship with Patti? Through the adventure, Mark learns about the need to belong and the gift of forgiveness.

Behind the Locked Door

Why does Mark's friend Whit keep his attic door locked? What's hidden up there? While staying with Whit, Mark grows curious when he's forbidden to go behind the locked door. It's a hard-learned lesson about trust and honesty.

Lights Out at Camp What-a-Nut

At camp, Mark finds out he's in the same cabin with Joe Devlin, Odyssey's biggest bully. And when Mark and Joe are paired in a treasure hunt, they plunge into unexpected danger and discover how God uses one person to help another.

The King's Quest

Mark is surprised and upset to find he must move back to Washington, D.C. He feels like running away. And that's exactly what The Imagination Station enables him to do! With Whit's help, he goes on a quest for the king to retrieve a precious ring. Through the journey, Mark faces his fears and learns the importance of obeying authority and striving for eternal things.

Danger Lies Ahead

Jack Davis knew he was off to a bad start when he saw a moving van in front of Mark's house, heard that an escaped convict could be headed toward Odyssey, and found himself in the principal's office—all on the first day of school! Thrown headfirst into the course of chaos, Jack's imagination runs overtime. Will it cost him his friendships with Oscar and Lucy?

Point of No Return

Turning over a new leaf isn't as easy as Jimmy Barclay thought it would be. And when his friends abandon him, his grandmother falls ill, and the only kid who seems to understand what he's going through moves away, he begins to wonder, *Does God really care?* Through the challenges, Jimmy discovers that standing up for what you believe in can be costly—and rewarding!

Dark Passage

When Matt and Jack discover a trap door in the yard at Whit's End, their curiosities get the best of them as The Imagination Station leads the pair back in time to the pre-Civil War South! And after Matt is mistaken for a runaway slave and sold at an auction, it's up to Jack to find and rescue him!

Other Works by the Author